Bridie O'Neill and Cathal's Ghost

Lizzie Collins

ISBN: 9798846287600

Chapter One
The Missing Leg

"Mam! Jimmy Dobson's leg's cut off. It was lying in the road – tore clean off. I saw it Mam! Mr. Feeney's cart ran right over it. When he pulled the horse up short it stepped back and ran over him again. It's cut clear off Mam!"

This was my brother Billy. He was eight years old and best known for an imagination which sometimes bordered on lies. Pa said he should write for the movies, which was laughable because he couldn't read or write.

Mam was cutting fat away from a piece of pork she'd managed to bargain for from a butcher on Dunbar Street. No-one shopped there willingly – there were flies everywhere and the meat was old and sometimes smelled. But if you had no money, you had no choice either.

Our mother sighed and fixed Billy with a fierce eye. Billy quailed – he knew her next move would be to cuff him round the ear

There was a sudden horrified scream, which even reached our fifth story tenement room. Mam dropped her knife and took the stairs to the street two at a time. Edith Dobson, Jimmy's mother, was one of her friends. They often walked together from our Manhattan home to press their noses against the windows of Bonwit's new store on Fifth Avenue, on a Sunday morning after chapel, where the Tenth Commandment had completely passed them by. The one about coveting – I think it's the tenth.

Mrs. Dobson had pulled her youngest boy Jimmy – Billy's playmate – onto the sidewalk. His disembodied leg could be quite clearly seen beneath the cart, the bloody end ragged, whereas my brother had said it had been cut clear off.

Jimmy was blue in the face and convulsing with shock. Then suddenly he collapsed against his mother's chest, his good right leg flopping over her arm, the toe of his scuffed shoe against the bloody pavement.

My mother hitched up her skirts and ran. Mrs. Dobson had stopped crying and was gazing with disbelief – yet to realize the child she had fed oatmeal to not ten minutes before had gone, his life's blood seeping through her dress. She looked at Mam, her face blank with shock.

But Rosie O'Neill wasn't fazed by much. While Billy and I cowered on the bottom step, she instructed Mr. Feeney to carry Jimmy home, Edith trailing behind hanging uselessly onto Jimmy's limp hand.

"Billy!" yelled Ma. "Go fetch Mr. Finkle – NOW!"

Police constable Ernie Finkelstein was the area officer assigned to the district of Dungannon Road. He arrived at a run huffing and panting, his cap under his arm and night-stick in his other hand. Mam gave him a minute to catch his breath, then grabbing me by the wrist and dragging me up the steps of the tenement next-but-one to our own, she hurried Mr. Finkle to the Dobson room.

I was terrified although I'd seen dead bodies – Mrs. Seigel in the next room to ours had died of the lung sickness the year before, but while she wheezed a lot, she was at least in possession of all her limbs. I'd helped Mam wrap her in an old sheet to be taken to a pauper's grave on Hart Island.

Mam with some difficulty, dragged her friend Edith into what served as the bedroom, behind a corner sectioned off with old planks, and helped her wash and change her clothes.

Mr. Finkle used my arrival to leave, taking Mr. Feeney to the station for questioning.

Once I was alone with Jimmy's body which had been laid out on the kitchen table, I leaned gingerly over and had a good look. He had bled out, so his lips were blue, his face white and there were smears of blood on his cheeks. He looked very patriotic.

What remained of the pants on his left leg had been ripped across to show his hip bone, but thankfully that was all. I tried not to look where half an hour before the rest of his leg had been, but I inadvertently glimpsed a piece of bone with tendons still attached, which looked like a chicken leg I'd once seen dressed.

I never did learn what happened to the bit in the street. In a part of the city where many people were starving, it didn't bear thinking about. Or perhaps I was a particularly gruesome ten-year-old, and ghastly imaginations ran in the family.

Chapter Two
Michael versus his Mam

My father was Robert – called Bob – O'Neill. His grandfather had brought his family to America to escape the Great Potato Famine, so dad was American-born.

Mam had come over from Ireland with her parents when she was about my own age. She drove us mad forever going on about the emerald green grass spread to the horizon. and the pretty country cottages, the handsome Irish boys, and dances on the village green. It hadn't done her grandparents' generation much good when they were pulling up their dinner from the fields, putrid from infected soil.

Then there was my fifteen-year-old brother Michael better known as Mick, and twins Sally and Kathleen, aged twelve. Not as many mouths to feed as most Irish American families, but then we were Protestants, not heathens like the other lot. Small family that we were, we still had two aunts, Polly and Dorothy – obviously known as Polly and Dolly - and my father's brother, Uncle Frank, who lived in the next street. We pooled whatever we had, and on the rare occasions there was anything over, we shared it with our neighbors.

Pa was a stevedore on the docks, but it was piecework so there wasn't a constant flow of money coming in. He would try to fill in between times by odd-jobbing, but as so many others were doing the same, and so few had money to spare, it was rarely enough. Gentle man though he was, he often sat brooding at home, lashing out at us kids from frustration.

Sometimes, when times were rough, Billy got into trouble for stealing bread or fruit from outside whatever shops were foolish enough to leave it there. He got caught by Finkle once, but the policeman turned the other way and pretended he hadn't seen.

It was different with Mick. He was a man grown. When he was caught shoplifting, Mr. Finkle banged him up in a cell. It scared the crap out of him.

Mam cried but there was no other way we could put food in our bellies. It broke Pa's heart when his son got on the wrong side of the law because he couldn't provide for us himself.

We mostly played in the streets. There were no parks in our part of the city – just endless rows of brick buildings.

We girls made rag dolls from scraps begged from our mothers or played hopscotch on the sidewalk. The boys had marbles or rigged ropes to the crossbars of streetlights to play 'carousel'. That's how poor Jimmy met his end. His hands slipped on the rope, and he ended under Dara Feeney's cart.

Then there were boys of Mick's age who hung about on tenement steps, laughing covertly amongst themselves and smoking cigarettes. Sometimes my brother was with them. My mother would skin him alive if she caught him with a cigarette in his mouth. By the surreptitious way he kept checking over his shoulder, he knew it too.

Mick liked girls. Luckily girls liked him too. He didn't need to hang about on street corners – he had other preoccupations. His steady girl was called Lilian Greenwood. Her dad owned an ironmongery three streets away. This made her quite a catch. It also made Mick unwelcome on Dean Street where they lived.

Lily Greenwood was considered a beauty. She had strawberry blonde hair she wore caught up with side combs hung with ribbons. She was a year older than Mick at sixteen and had large bosoms, a tiny waist and a way of looking at the boys through long, silky eyelashes that seemed to stupefy them. I noticed she also had a habit of opening the top two buttons on her blouse as she skipped out of her door. In short, Lily was not at all proper, no matter what her doting father thought. My mother said, 'she was no better than she should be' and sniffed.

Mick might not be getting into bother with the older boys then, but some of those idiots even had guns they kept well hidden in their pockets, which always seemed stupid to me. What if they went off accidentally? There'd be a few less kids born on the Lower East Side if that happened.

Anyway, Mick caught it when Kitty saw him with Lily up Carter's Yard, and her with her skirt bunched round her waist and her hair all messy. Kathleen saw her big brother with his hands where they'd no business being. The kissing was… enthusiastic, said our Kathleen. I'd no idea what she meant.

Regrettably for Michael, of us all Kitty was the worst gossip. She went straight to Mam and tittle-tattled what she'd seen. I only knew because I was using the can behind the bedroom wall.

Mam fetched her a hefty whack for telling tales, then ran outside where they must have heard her on Staten Island. She took a deep, deep breath, inflated her lungs, opened her mouth and let rip. I took the steps two at a time behind her, ready for the entertainment to come.

"MICHAEL CULLEN O'NEILLLL! Get your arse in here. And don't you pretend you can't hear me. If I've to come looking for you, they'll be searching for what's left under the Brooklyn Bridge!"

I swear the whole of New York held its breath.

As our Michael sloped round the corner from the direction of Dean Street, the road emptied and the tenement windows filled as if for a tickertape parade.

Our Mick must have topped six foot by then – he was always well-grown – and Mam was a tiny doll-like woman who just about came to his shoulder. Yet she scared the crap out of all of us – and half the neighbors as well.

She reached up and grabbed him by the hair in front of his ear – the bit that really hurts and you can't get free from. By this time, she was speechless with fury as she hauled him upstairs.

She dragged one of our two chairs out from under the table with her foot, and plonked him down on it, then slapped him so hard it left a palm print on his cheek.

"Have I not told you you mutton-head – if I catch you with that Greenwood trollop again your father'll take his belt to

your bare rump? Seems you thought I was joking."
She tugged at his hair until the rest of his face matched her
palm print.

This was the point at which my unassuming mild-mannered
father chose to appear on the scene. He glanced
heavenward. Rosie O'Neill in full flow needed a whole host
of angels to control her, and that he didn't have, so he gave
Sally five cents and a jug, and told her to get herself down
to the Shamrock and ask Mr. Kelly to fill it up. Mr. Kelly
of course would be expecting her. He wasn't deaf.But Pa
was too late. Mother was out of the door and headed for
Dean Street where she caught Burt Greenwood closing up
his shop for the day. He turned, smiling. Then saw this
creature from his worst nightmare, sleeves shoved up, arms
akimbo, spitting fire from her eyes. He took a couple of
steps backwards.

"And where's that slut daughter of yours? I guess you won't
be knowing what she's up to with my damned – for damned
he surely is – son in Carter's Yard?"

She spat on the pavement at Greenwood's feet and his face
creased with distaste. He was English-born and hated the
Irish as much as they hated him.

Just at that moment Lily had the misfortune to walk out of
the shop, blouse done up, skirt pulled down, looking as if
butter wouldn't melt in her mouth.

My mother fetched her an almighty whack across the face
and Mr. Greenwood sent for Mr. Finkelstein who given the
number of guffawing bystanders, was obliged to lift a

kicking and struggling Mam by the waist and lock her up, at least until she calmed down.

Pa drank the beer.

Chapter Three
Unexpected Death and Abrupt Departure

As Jimmy's fate showed, death was no stranger on the streets of the poverty-stricken parts of New York. Pa, who was always polite and well-spoken, was fortunate enough to land full-time work as a mechanic in a cotton mill, rebuilt after the great fire. He loved it until his arm was crushed to the elbow in a loom and had to be amputated. He couldn't work after that and couldn't provide for us. The foreman swore at the blood, because they'd to reset the weft, which on a jacquard loom such as theirs could take a long time.

It was me who found my father hanging by his leather belt from a meat hook he'd screwed into a bedroom joist, neck broke and blue tongue hanging from the corner of his mouth. When Michael and I couldn't lift him down, we'd to fetch Mr. O'Keefe from downstairs to help.

Some years later, Mick had survived the Great War, only to die of influenza weeks after disembarkation. Sally was married with a newborn and lived with her husband in Brooklyn, and Kitty was an overlooker in charge of three looms. It was thanks to her wages and Pa's meagre savings we could move to better living quarters, with a proper bedroom and a flushing toilet. As there was now fresh water, albeit cold, from a wooden tank on the roof, I appeared to change color overnight.

My light brown hair, after thorough washing, turned out to be not only less itchy, but a shining profusion Mam plaited and wound it round my head like a crown. A worn dress I'd always taken to be soft beige with pink sprigs on it, turned out to be pale blue scattered with forget-me-nots.

One bright blue sunny morning, on one of the increasingly few periods Mam wasn't behind bars during Prohibition, an automobile cab chugged past sidewalks on our dilapidated street and pulled up on our block. I threw up the window for a better look. Morgan Allen wolf-whistled. I put out my tongue.

Of course, we'd seen plenty of cars downtown, autobuses even, but very few made it to our neck of the woods.

A strange little man in a tight sweater and loose pants jumped out and instructed the cabbie to wait. The cabbie turned down his 'For Hire' sign again.

The stranger checked out the numbers painted in white next to each door and located our tenement at number twenty-three, I'd never seen him before but my mother seemed to be expecting him.

"Mrs. O'Neill." he said to Mam, who wobbled slightly, and for one awful moment I thought she was about to curtsy, but she hiccoughed instead.

"I'm Hugh Brady Mrs. O'Neill. I'm sent to collect Bridget as arranged with Mr. Cullen."

'WHAT!! Collect me…. COLLECT ME! What the hell was going on here?'

The man jogged up the steps after Mam and I trailed behind.

"Sit yourself down, Mr. Brady. Will you take tea?" said Rosie O'Neill, my mother, indicating by gesture I should go to the bedroom out of the way. As I left, she busied herself with the kettle. Mr. Brady offered no further conversation that I could hear.

Within five minutes Mam was standing sternly over me, hands on hips like in the old days.

"Mr. Brady has been paid by my brother Colin to take you back to Ireland. This is what your Pa wanted, so keep your mouth shut for once, Bridie O'Neill. If you stayed here, he thought you might end up a whore like Lily Greenwood's set on being, or dead of disease like Mick. Sally has a husband to support her and Kitty has a paying job which leaves you. I can't support you and pay the rent – '*it was Kitty's wage did that*' – I'm getting no younger," she said, tucking the bottle away in her apron pocket.

"You're not a bad looker so you should find an Irish lad right enough. In the meantime you're to go work on your uncle Colin's farm in Wicklow. You'll like it," she finished half-heartedly.

"Colin Cullen? You can't be serious."

She cuffed me for my cheek.

"He thinks the same, which is why the world knows him as Connell Cullen." '*and that's better, how?*' "He's the oldest of us and didn't want to leave, so Da sold some of the stock and made the house and the rest over to him when we made the crossing."

She tied my hair back with a blue kerchief, pinched my cheeks to make them rosy, then dragged me out to be introduced to Hugh Brady, who took me by the shoulders and turned me round, examining me as if I was a prize heifer.

I'll say this for my mother, she didn't hang about. She tugged a carpet bag with every stitch of clothing I possessed from under her bed and handed it to Brady, then pulled on my one and only coat, taking an involuntary step backwards.

I was marched back down to the taxi. I passed Daniel Boyle, Kenny O'Keefe, Morgan Allen who had the grace to look crest-fallen, Davy O'Connor, Lilian Greenwood, my sisters Sally and Kitty and Aunties Polly and Dolly. No Uncle Frank or Billy though. There was Edith Dobson, mother of Jimmy who died with only the one leg. It's surprising just how many people will turn up to watch a catastrophe in the making.

My Mam kissed me on the forehead and told me not to be a stranger - she'd clearly been at the bottle again. She patted my cheek as she shoved me into the cab. I never saw her again.

It wasn't until the automobile was pulling through the back streets, and I was watching the dirty tenements turn into smarter houses with iron railings, that I thought to wonder why I was going to Ireland and not on to Kansas or Tennessee or any other of the forty-eight states which comprised North America. Sure, Rosie O'Neill intended never to set eyes on me again.

Chapter Four
Land of Blood and Bounty

Hugh Brady wasn't so bad – I'd known worse. I was fifteen – past old enough to cope with a slap on the arse, so we got on okay on the way to Ireland – apart from the sea-sickness. He spent more time holding a pail to my chin than fancying my bosoms, and I think he was past relieved when we sighted the southern tip of Ireland. Myself, I cared neither one way nor the other.

Uncle Connell had paid him to collect me, he and his family being otherwise engaged in business.

So it was with a face to match, I first set eyes on the Emerald Isle, land of my ancestors. Hugh carried my bag and his in one hand and hauled me to the immigration shack by the arm. To say Dublin had such a huge harbor, it had very little by way of paperwork when it came to getting in. Perhaps that's because everyone was trying to get out.

Further round the jetties, stevedores by the dozen were operating cranes which swung huge packing-cases and barrels from cargo ships onto the dock-side – I could hear them cursing from where I stood.

We were hours in New York getting on the boat – it seemed we were only a half-hour getting off. Soon enough, a skinny man with grey whiskers and a bent nose, glanced arbitrarily at papers signed by my uncle, and banged a large stamp saying 'IN' and the date in the required box, then waved us through with his thumb, not once looking up.

Once outside, Hugh tipped his hat at the driver of a cart pulled by a bored-looking brown piebald horse. It swished its tail to keep off the flies and chomped at the bit, then on instruction moved forwards at a clop.

"Mornin' to thee, Hugh" said a ruddy-cheeked driver in belt and braces.

"And a right fine mornin' it is, Charlie."

Hugh slung both bags into the cart, jumped aboard, hoisted me up and plonked me down on one of the planks which ran the length of the cart on both sides, serving as rudimentary seats. By this point in time, my mood might be described as shell-shocked.

"Hup!" directed the driver and the cart lurch forward.

We headed south through the farmlands of County Wicklow, past beautiful verdant mountains and crystal waterfalls. We were greeted very occasionally by smaller rigs heading towards Dublin, the occupants of which turned and studied me curiously. I wondered at the hostility in their gaze. I was a young girl with flaxen plaits and a dress as shabby as any of their own if not a little shorter.

"You'd best be on your guard and keep your mouth shut until folks know who y'are," warned Brady. "We're not long Irish. Until a few years ago we were still English lackies. Any foreign-accent speaking English might be misunderstood. Being near the new border with the north, Wicklow came in for some special treatment. Many a mother lost her husband and sons in the fighting."

New York this wasn't. Hoodlums looked like bad guys on Dungannon Road. This landscape was stunningly beautiful and peaceful, the loudest sound the melodious trill of

15

blackbirds flitting from branch to branch on the rowan trees which lined the track.

It was high summer, ocean-crossings being inadvisable over the colder months, and the land was a cornucopia of blessings. We passed whitewashed cottages with gardens rich with carrot and beet tops, raspberry canes and scarlet-flowered beans on tall trellises, and fruit trees with drifts of pink and white blossoms scattered on the earth beneath.

A lady in a white kerchief and an old-fashioned long skirt handed us a wicker bowl of strawberries as we passed, and wished us good day, glancing fearfully at me as she stood back from the cart.

"Annie O'Brien's husband was shot dead by a Black and Tan in front of her very face," said Hugh as we rode along.

"What's a Black and Tan?"

"English assassins posing as police," he said, and spat over the side of the cart. The driver grunted his agreement.

"Bastairds!" he said.

"We have to look forward to a bright and beautiful free Ireland," smiled Hugh Brady enthusiastically.

"Even if they've penned the Protestant heathens north of the border. We'll be fine as long as they don't start poking their long English-loving snouts down here."

This was my first understanding of why it was wise to keep your mouth shut in Ireland. It was puzzling why Rosie Cullen O'Neill should be such an ardent Protestant, yet her brother clung to the Catholic faith. Perhaps that's why she was in New York and he was still in the 'Old Country'.

The narrow mountain lane broadened as we headed ever southwards and soon, on either side of the road were far-flung green meadows, some scattered with wildflowers, others with fine horses, satin-flanked and maned, kicking up their hooves.

"Those are your uncle's mares," said Hugh, sucking on a strawberry.

It sure was difficult to imagine Annie O'Brien watching her husband's blood soaking his front yard amid the vegetables and flowers – or gunshots shattering the perfect peace.

Chapter Five

A Plethora of Cousins and the Birth of Bridie Cullen

It seemed hours since we'd climbed aboard Charlie Kevan's cart at Dublin docks. My arse was numb from the jolting of the cart over ruts in the dirt road, even though I'd bunched my skirt up cushion-like.

Hugh told me I could thank all the angels in heaven the weather was dry, and the cart not struggling through mud to the axles, with us knee-deep pushing.

Nevertheless, I was relieved when the cart took a turn and Charlie jumped down to open a five-bar gate into a busy yard,

Compared to the quaint cottages we'd passed on the road, Uncle Connell's farm was a mansion. Not that the house itself was anything exceptional, but the large stable building, open to show its hayloft, and various assorted pig pens, hen runs and byres which surrounded it, expanded its appearance considerably.

"Here come's your uncle now", said Hugh raising his voice above the cacophony.

A vigorous man, perhaps in his fifties was striding across the yard towards us. He'd that tough 'man of the land' look about him, skin tanned by wind and sun, hair tangled, eyes bright and far-seeing.

"Welcome t'Long Barrow", said my uncle raising a sinewy arm to help me down.

He smiled so broadly I had to reciprocate.

18

Half-running along in his wake was a plump woman with bright rosy cheeks, tying her hair up into a kerchief. She looked harassed. But when she finally reached me, she knocked her husband out of the way:

"Sorry, husband…Let me to her!"

Uncle Connell stepped back grinning widely.

"Bridget, this is your aunt Siobhan. She's full of it today – she's been leanin' out of that window since day-break!" said Uncle Connell

"I'd rather you called me Bridie, Bridie O'Neill's my name," I said in my best polite manner.

"Sure we will – if you'll call me Conn. Real name's Colin. Didn't like that, so I took my mother's name Connell – she was from down south in Cork. My pub pals choked on their beer at Connell Cullen…. so – Conn it is. I'm your Uncle Conn, Miss Bridie O'Neill."

He was suddenly serious and gave Aunt Siobhan a sidewards glance.

"We'll need to fix that,"

"Come away in, *cailin og*… let's get you settled."

She grabbed my bag from Hugh and told him by gesture to remove himself. Uncle Conn chuckled.

"Your Aunt is in charge – only indoors, mind."

There was a defensive edge to his voice which gave me the impression Auntie was in charge of more than just the house.

The farmhouse was a typical long homestead constructed of drystone, whitewashed. A thatched roof, of course, very neatly done. Uncle Conn was clearly a man of some means – he'd enough for one fare to New York and two back, and a cart to haul us from the docks.

The interior of the farmstead was at first pitch black and it took a while for my eyes to adjust to the gloom.

Seven children, the oldest boy looking about my own age - stood almost to attention, oldest to youngest I assumed although there was a girl appreciably taller than her brother in the middle. All looked thoroughly scrubbed and dressed neat and clean. I'd just got off a boat, been unable to keep food down for a week, and suddenly felt completely overwhelmed.

Aunt Siobhan caught me as I fell. I came to almost as soon as I hit the stone-flagged floor and climbed to my feet scarlet with embarrassment.

"Dan – take Cousin Bridie's bag. Molly, she'll be in your bed – you can share with Rosheen and Rosie tonight. Rosheen, help her off with those soiled clothes – she can use one of your nighties until she gets sorted.."

Daniel, Rosheen, Sean, Molly, Ronan, Craig and Rosie. I didn't remember a one.

To describe their attributes would take an age so I'll work them into the story. I got to know them soon enough.

"Tomorrow will do right enough for talking my darlin'. Now get you off and rest. Rosie – look after your cousin."

So I was put into Molly's clean, soft bed, the like of which I'd never known in my whole life, and within seconds I was drowned in sleep too black for dreams. I didn't even rouse to the smell of frying bacon.

It was eight o'clock when I awoke.

Rosie was sitting on the bottom of the bed, chin propped against her raised knee, crunching on an apple.

"We thought you was dead," she said without preamble. "Do New York folks always sleep so late?"

She leaned closer and examined my face:

"Pasty, aren't you? I've done my morning chores – I look after the hens and collect the eggs. Mam says you're to get up or you'll miss breakfast."

She skipped to the door, tossed her chestnut curls and yelled:

"SSSEEEEAAAANNNNNN! She's up – fetch the water," followed by a cheeky "and be sharp about it." which was a dead-on copy of her mother.

As she left, she turned and eyed me seriously.

"I'm six," she said.

Sean, small and solemn with freckles and spectacles, deposited the bowl of water and left, turning his head so as not to see me in my nightdress.

I took my forget-me-not dress out of my bag and flattened it out with my palms. It was still creased, but it was the best

I could do. I brushed out my hair and tied it back with one of my two satin ribbons.

I'd come from a home where the chance of a meal of any kind was not to be relied on. That morning I sat down to farm fare – Rosie's eggs, bacon cut from a fitch above the hearth, mushrooms from the field by the river and black pudding which I loved. Molly told me the English called it 'blood pudding' and why. It wasn't quite so appetizing after that.

I liked Molly although there were times I couldn't understand a word she said. She had a habit of switching into the Irish language in the middle of a sentence. Rosie said knowledgeably that she was 'bi-lingeral' which made Molly laugh.

On the very first day, Siobhan lined the kids up again and took me to one side. Conn eyed them all one after the other.

"What you hear now you will never repeat or all the devils in hell will be on your tail – do you understand me?"

Rosie and Craig, the two youngest, looked petrified.

"Father Lynch – never was a man so deserving of his name - has been threatening them with hell and damnation for as long as they can remember, evil old goat!" sniffed my aunt.

Conn glared at her and she folded her arms and glared back.

"O'Neill is a name from across the new border so you'll not use it," Conn said to me. "These are troubled times and your accent will mark you out. Its near enough English that some won't know the difference. From now on you're to be

Bridie Cullen. The name holds some sway in these parts," he finished with pride.

So Bridie Cullen I was from then on.

Chapter Six
Aidan, Dempsey and Lorelei

It was three years before Bridie Cullen reached the top of the farm tree. Aunt Siobhan said I'd done it double quick but my knowledge of housework was lacking.

In those three years I'd written Mam twice. She replied neither time. She couldn't read and write herself but Kitty could, and Sally at a push. Perhaps I'd drop by someday in a posh frock and pearl earrings.

In those three short years I'd taken Rosie's job with the hens. She took great delight in showing me how to muck out the runs and introduced me to Boru, the rooster – vicious creature. I'd also learned that pigs stink, and so did I after an hour in their company; cows are amongst the stupidest, most inquisitive and heaviest creatures on the planet.

I had eventually learned to milk them and was more careful after one stepped on my foot and broke three bones. Danny said I was stupid to put my foot under a cow's hoof.

I'd watched Daniel breaking colts in the paddock of course, but I didn't fall in love with horses until I met Gealach – Moonlight – literally face to face.

As Daniel and Rosheen had their own mounts, Uncle Conn decided I should too.

He introduced me to the horse by locking us together in a stall. He figured we'd get to know each other one way or another. I stroked her nose trying not to look at the teeth beneath, she nuzzled my hand and a friendship was born.

Gealach wasn't a baby – she was six years old – but she had a calm manner and took care of me as I learned to ride. I only fell off twice. Rosie and Rosheen laughed so hard it made me cry, and I vowed never to do it again. Danny grinned to himself and chewed a straw – which was even worse.

I also learned to love my cousins – all except Sean who never loosened up and never stopped treating me like a guest. Rosheen said he'd always been like that – he'd come round. But three years on he still eyed me with caution.

I was now eighteen and was beginning to turn heads. My rose-gold hair, streaked bright by outdoor living, hung down below my waist and my breasts would have done Lily Greenwood proud.

Daniel was a clear illustration of Mam's Irish boy, with his tanned skin, bright green eyes and a mouth always turned up in a smile. He'd the typical Irish build, slight but sinewy and strong. Many a local girl had her eye on him and his Da's farm.

His closest friend was Aidan Valentine, whose father's farmlands abutted Uncle Conn's. He sat his Irish thoroughbred like a true champion and could make it rear and prance with a nudge of his heel. He cut a dashing and romantic figure in high boots and fitted jacket which showed off his broad shoulders. And for some reason he seemed to think I was worth his while and took to calling me Lorelei.

 There were sour remarks and nudges from a few of the local girls who despite my Cullen name, saw me as an interloper. Uncle Conn had had the right of it when he renamed me, but it didn't solve my problems altogether.

Disaster came about one day while Aidan was doing his party trick with Dempsey, his beloved horse. As the animal shuffled backwards, he bumped into little Meggie Doyle and she ended up under a back hoof.

Mary Doyle stood screaming at her door while her husband Joe put a bullet through Dempsey's head.

It made no difference – Meggie lived, but in the short span allotted her, never walked again.

Uncle Conn became arbiter and finally persuaded Joe Doyle and Aidan's father, Niall Valentine to come to terms over payment for Meggie's care, and a sum to compensate Joe for the loss of her labor, which came to quite a tidy sum, even though the poor mite herself perished within a twelve-month.

Next day, Aunt Siobhan sent me up to the pasture with a basket of food for Daniel. I saddled Gealach and ambled along lanes and through meadows until I saw two figures in a distant field.

Aidan had walked the six miles from his home to see Danny and was dusty and perspiring from the exercise. I watched Daniel take his friend by the arm and hug him. They'd grown up together and were as close as brothers.

Aidan took off his jacket and wiped damp curls from his forehead, then picked up hammer and nails from Daniel's tool pack and beat out some of his grief fixing a length of broken fencing. He ended up throwing hammer and nails to the ground and covering his face with his hands.

Daniel tried to comfort him but he just pushed him away and, figuring Aidan needed his own space he went back to his work.

I waited a while, then quietly tied Gealach to a fence post, spread a linen cloth on the ground and set out the food I'd packed for Daniel picnic-style, inviting Aidan to sit with me.

At first, he just turned away – to compose himself I supposed – but then came and sat, silently studying the grass between his outstretched legs.

Much to my surprise, he slumped sideways, buried his head in the crook of my neck and wept. It was embarrassing, but I was warming to the idea of cuddling up to him. Eventually he leaned back again and examined my face carefully saying:

"Thank you, Lorelei. Thank you, thank you."

The kiss he gave me in thanks started off brotherly and ended anything but. We lay back on the grass, but when his hands began to rove over my body like Mick's with Lily Greenwood, I knew it was time to leave.

Crimson-faced, I picked up my basket and four corners of the cloth with food and all, and scampered down the hillside.

When I reached the road, I glanced back. Aidan was still standing where I'd left him, watching.

Chapter Seven
An Ill-starred Proposal

One Saturday evening not long after, the church in nearby Cordonagh held one of the dances Mam was so full of enthusiasm for.

A wooden floor was laid on the village green, surrounded by a frame wreathed with bright mountain flowers, collected in baskets and woven into long garlands by the older girls.

The day began with games for the small children and ended with dancing to flute, pipes and drum. As night drew on and the stars began to show in the darkening sky, flares were lit and lanterns hung from hooked poles.

I thought of Manhattan and was glad I'd come.

I linked arms and spun first with Daniel. Then, as the music grew faster and wilder, laughed through a series of partners until I stopped dead before Aidan Valentine. His face was an unreadable mask but his fingers clenching my arms were painful. I tried to knock him away but he only held tighter.

Daniel was the first to notice what was happening and arrived just as Aidan swung back his hand to hit me across the face.

Daniel grabbed his wrist and pulled him away so hard Aidan stumbled.

"Go home, Aidan," he threatened. "All here can see you're worse for the whisky. If you go now, we'll laugh about it come morning."

"You defending this little English slut, Cullen? She's no cousin of yours."

He faced up to Daniel, pushing at him. Danny punched him on the nose, which spirted red down Aidan's rumpled white shirt, then he launched himself at my cousin but missed. Danny sidestepped, and Aidan landed flat on his face on the wooden floor.

Both fathers dragged their sons apart. Niall threw a punch to Aidan's jaw that knocked him to the ground:

"Come away and leave the ¹*cailin* alone, fool – but first you will offer Mr. Cullen an apology."

Niall hauled Aidan upright by his coat collar and when he didn't speak, shook him like a terrier with a rat.

"Say it, or I'll give you the beating you deserve."

Aidan's mother and Aunt Siobhan stood hand in hand on the edge of the dance floor, white as sheets.

"I beg your forgiveness, Conn Cullen, for the disrespect to your family," Aidan said sullenly.

"Appears to me ²*buachaill*, the apology should go to the lady," said Conn.

He pulled me forward and when Aidan and I stood face to face he just crumpled, now stone cold sober and embarrassed beyond bearing at his behavior.

The silence around us was deafening, the crowd agog to see what would happen next.

Tears coursing down his face, Aidan said quietly:

"I do most sincerely beg your pardon, Bridie-Lorelei. It had been my intention to ask your uncle for your hand, but since the…. accident I am not the Aidan Valentine I have always tried to be."

Believe it or not, the only thing I could think of to say was:

"And I am Daniel's cousin but I'm not English – I'm from New York in America. I'm a New Yorker and we pushed the English out too."

I strode off home in high dudgeon, and Aunt Siobhan recovered herself enough to get the band playing again before she ran after me.

The last thing I saw was Daniel leading the other boys in a somewhat disco-ordinated Irish jig. Niall Valentine had hauled his son off home in disgrace.

"Well, I have to say," sniffed Aunt Siobhan, "I've heard better proposals."

It was only then it sank in what had happened. The most eligible bachelor in the county had offered for me, and instead of accepting I'd told him I was from New York. I looked at my aunt aghast and she burst out laughing.

"Sure, if he's worth having he'll ask again. Let's hope you're not the one addled with the drink when he does, or the Lord above knows what will happen. You'll probably give him the laundry list."

Dan and Uncle Conn were full of concern when they returned at the end of the evening. They'd stayed on to play down any bad feeling. There had been an atmosphere but it was soon dispelled.

"Oh, I'm okay," I said at their distress. "At least my head won't ache in the morning. And I straightened out the English thing once and for all."

I rushed through my chores the following morning and found Daniel in the stables cleaning tack. I kissed his cheek and said:

"Thanks, cousin, for your help last night, but I was surprised Aidan's pain is all for his horse and not the little girl whose life hangs in the balance – or her family."

Dan was quiet for a while, then put down the tin of saddle soap and cloth he was using.

"You've been here for a matter of years now, but in some ways you're still a city girl. You must have noticed to people like me and Aidan, our horses are friends, travelling companions and a source of pride for our care and skill in raising and training them.

"Aiden raised Dempsey from a colt. You've seen how well he could perform at Aidan's command.."

"I didn't know you had a special horse as well. Why have I never seen it?"

"He died the year you came – broke his leg and Da put a bullet in his brain like Dempsey."

For a moment his eyes moistened and he wiped his face angrily on his sleeve.

"I was just like Aidan. I got drunk; I hit out at Rosheen in temper - she still has a scar on her chin which shames me every time I see it. But I was fifteen so had no girl I loved enough to offer for. He won't forgive himself easily."

I could feel the tears prick at my own eyes.

"What can I do?"

"Nothing. You're too young."

"But I can't lie just to comfort him."

He paused for a moment to mull things over, then shook his head.

"You need to speak to Mam. She makes a lot of noise but most of it makes sense."

He picked up the saddle soap and returned to his task adding:

"It'll all come right in the end – it always does one way or another."

I thought to myself his mother wasn't the only wise person in this family.

¹ girl ² boy

Chapter Eight
A Budding Flower

I told Aunt Siobhan what Daniel had said when we spoke of Aidan in the stable.

Aunty agreed with Dan. I was far too young in the head to even consider marriage. What's more, she thought Eefa Valentine would be horrified at the thought of her only son marrying when he was not yet twenty-three. He'd yet to make a man's reputation in the world.

My aunt went on to say I'd have been better to keep my mouth shut about being from New York as well. The village was very on edge after Meggie's injury and it wouldn't take much for them to round on the Cullens as well, them being so close with the Valentines.

"This puts you in a quandary," said my aunt. "I think it would be better if either you or Aidan removed yourselves for a while until folks forget."

"You could always marry Aidan," broke in Rosheen, who'd been snooping in the background. "That'd give Mary O'Dowd something to think about. She follows him around like a shadow."

I pushed the conversation to the back of my mind, and as it was a good warm afternoon I took the opportunity to get myself thoroughly cleaned up. I carried all my clothes to the river, soaped them then rinsed and beat them as near dry as possible against stones on the banking before tossing them over nearby bushes to dry.

I'd pulled one or two little jumping things from my hair in recent days, so I stripped off and plunged in, ducking my head beneath the water until my hair floated loose against its ripples.

To dry off, I sat on a smooth boulder, its surface pleasantly warm against my bottom, and began to comb out my hair strand by strand, until it dried, glistening gold in the sun.

It was then –how could I have been so stupid – I found my clothes were missing. It didn't take long to discover the culprits. Rosie had dragged the stolid Craig, Uncle Conn's right-hand 'man', into her schemes and they'd raced off down the field scattering the damp clothes as they ran. I could hear Rosie's giggle all the way to the road.

It was fortunate I found my underwear pretty quickly, my blouse as well, as it was Uncle Conn who found me. He lifted me up so I could dislodge my skirt from the side of a hawthorn bush. I was scarlet with mortification.

When we got back and Aunt Siobhan learned of the afternoon's work from a defiant Rosie, I was pleased to see my youngest cousin put over her mother's knee, and her bottom well and truly warmed with the bread paddle propped on the hearth.

Craig had already made himself scarce. Uncle Conn said he'd be back of the pig pen because nobody in their right mind would go there.

It soon became apparent, that Aidan's behavior at the dance, and these superficially harmless escapades, had brought my aunt and uncle's worries to a head.

Auntie said I was now a young woman with a young woman's body and a snare to any young man who came my way. Daniel didn't help matters by giving a loud whistle.

But when the subject of my leaving - even temporarily - was broached more seriously, my tears came and wouldn't stop.

I excused myself after supper and went to walk the pastures behind the yard. The hens had gone to roost and the cows taken to the byre, so it was quieter than usual.

I could understand why my Cullen family wanted to see the back of me. I was living in a house with five males, two of them grown enough to understand my aunt's point of view.

I knew Conn and Siobhan would be devastated to lose me. They were my true parents and cared for me in a way Rosie and Bob O'Neill never had. They would do whatever they could to help me, but it was up to me to come to a decision about my intentions.

"Please Auntie, before you make more plans, I need to speak to Aidan," I said. "I don't want him to think this is all his fault. I have to explain and hope he'll understand…." my voice tailed off.

"That would be kind," agreed my uncle seriously. "I'll speak to Niall."

"No, I think Aidan would be less embarrassed if as few people as possible knew about it."

Daniel arranged a meeting at a hay meadow between the two farms, and I asked Auntie to keep tabs on Rosheen and

Rosie. I was early. A tall, long-legged laborer was scything the edge of the field furthest from the road,

While I was waiting and wondering what on earth I was going to say, I idly picked dog-daisies from the grass and twisted them into a garland, which I tossed over the wall when I noticed Aidan tying his father's gelding to a nearby gate-post.

He dropped to the ground at my side and turned to look at me, shocking me with the pain in his eyes.

"Oh, don't grieve Aidan, please," I pleaded. "I promise you, you and I are as good friends as we ever were."

He managed a tentative smile

"You and I have come to terms, and you'll just have to brazen it out with the Doyles. Come and talk to Daniel – he's forking hay in the loft - while I saddle Gealach. We'll ride through Cordonagh together. Then they'll see you and I at least have made up. Perhaps we could call at the Doyles and offer our sympathy. I'll take some of auntie's fudge for Meggie."

If further proof were needed that I was too naïve for marriage this was it. In retrospect, I couldn't believe I could have been so stupid.

Chapter Nine

Hard Lessons All Round and an Unexpected Act of Generosity

The ride to Cordonagh under any other circumstances would have been perfect.

The Irish countryside was at its splendid best. We rode side by side down the country road but as we neared the village, I noticed Aidan's hands tighten on the reins and his back straighten. By the time we passed the first houses, he was staring stiffly ahead.

The villagers, at first disinterested became increasingly hostile. As we neared Joe Doyle's house, they began throwing things. Gealach reared in panic and I was almost unseated. Aidan grabbed my reins and galloped as fast as he dare behind the nearest building.

Fortuately, one of the local kids saw the chance of a shiny silver sixpence and hightailed it down the road to Long Barrow.

When he heard what had happened, and the danger had been not only to Aidan but to his niece, Conn took his shotgun down from over the mantle, filled his pocket full of ammunition, saddled up and rode towards the village. Auntie Siobhan had done her best to restrain him but he pushed her aside roughly as he strode through the door.

"Rosheen!" hissed her mother, "ride to 'Redmile' and fetch Niall Valentine. Daniel and Sean load the old shotguns in the barn - I just hope the damn things haven't seized up.

And pray to the Lord Jesus, if there's a death it's not Cullen or Valentine writ on the certificate.

"Aidan's going to get himself killed – Conn too, likely. Go! GO!" she cried and slapped Rosheen's horse on the rump.

The end result was Conn, Daniel and Sean rode out of the village like Gary Cooper bound for Arizona. They were joined by Niall and Rosheen, the latter looking more dangerous than any of them, green eyes narrowed, Titian locks thrown back from her face.

Thankfully no blood was spilled that day but it was a close thing.

Although a potentially deadly situation, it did serve one purpose. Aidan could appreciate everyone's safety would be best served if I left quietly.

My speech too, although it had softened from my broad Yankee brogue, was still decidedly American. I would always be a foreigner to the villagers.

After Aidan and Niall had ridden through the gate and down the road home, Conn, Daniel, Siobhan and I sat round the scrubbed kitchen table. Molly and Rosheen, the latter a young girl - even if a gun-totin' one - sat silent next to the fire.

Several ideas on how to remove me safely from 'Long Barrow' were put forward and discarded.

Some other place in Ireland was suggested – Dublin perhaps, or Belfast – but I would have been no better off. In the one there'd be problems with the English; in the other with the Irish, and as I had an accent foreign to both, I could be in trouble either way.

"You could always go back to New York," mused Aunt Siobhan. "You've family there. Surely they'll put you up until you can sort yourself out."

This was the worst idea I'd ever heard. I thought of the cramped one bed-roomed apartment, the smog-ridden air and the bullies on the streets and I recoiled.

If I went back there, could I get out again? I couldn't stay there now I'd smelled honeysuckle on the breeze; or toasted my toes against a roaring fire while the wind blew snow against the windows.

Auntie Siobhan read the expression on my face rightly.

"To be sure, you'll not be going back as you came. Not the ragged little skeleton with the white face who walked over that stoop three years ago. You'll go home with a coat on your back and food in your belly or my name's not Siobhan Nolan Cullen."

Uncle Conn rocked back on his chair a grin on his face.

"It'll be your own children's heritage you'll be dibbing into then, Siobhan Nolan Cullen?"

"Bridie's as much our child as any of the others – that's the truth of the matter."

To my utter amazement it was Sean who stepped forward to interrupt the grown-ups. He stood tall and straight and announced:

"Bridie is my sister – she can have half of whatever will come to me."

It seemed everyone was as shocked as I was, because for a few moments there was absolute silence, during which time Sean began to fidget, and glanced from one face to another as if expecting a challenge.

Aunt Siobhan stood up, knocking over her chair in the process, and grasped her child to her bosom repeating over and over:

"It's a saint we've raised Conn Cullen. A miracle of a *wain*!"

Sean pushed her away, embarrassed in the way of boys confronted with too much emotion.

Not to be outdone, Rosheen chimed in her consent too. The others nodded their agreement and a little voice from a bedroom yelled:

"Mine, too!" Clearly Rosie had had her ear to the door.

"Looks like you're family whether you like it or not, Bridget Cullen," said Danny.

"Bridie."

"Or Lorelei," laughed my oldest brother. "By my reckoning, if we all give you half of our inheritances you'll be three times richer than each of the rest of us."

The room went silent while everyone thought that through.

"Sure, it's a true Irishman you are Daniel Cullen." concluded his mother wryly.

Rosheen talked her way into accompanying her mother and me to Dublin on a shopping trip. I'd thought to buy a coat for warmth on the journey; perhaps some sturdier shoes or hair ribbons but I'd underestimated Auntie Siobhan.

It wasn't until we were in Clerys' in Dublin trying on dresses, coats, skirts – even hats – that I suddenly realized my uncle was not just an ordinary farmer, but a man of some considerable means.

I looked at Rosheen – truly a stunning beauty with her shining hair and perfect complexion and saw her for the first time. I was used to her baggy overalls and yard boots but it suddenly came to me she'd look like a princess in a coal sack.

And the others too. Daniel – every girls idea of Prince Charming – kind and considerate and so good looking; Molly academic and clever; Sean, serious and with a compassion which had amazed us all; Ronan who could sing like a bird and keep perfect time on a bodhran drum; Craig, farmer in the making, whose skill at husbandry and care for his animals was making him a respected member of the farming community, not yet in his teens. And lastly little Rosie – now 10 years old – with her chestnut curls, rosy cheeks and indomitable spirit.

Now I knew their worth, I was about to lose every one of them.

Chapter Ten
A Gift and a Promise For Lorelei

Aidan Valentine. Now there was a real problem. I'd become very fond of him and knew my feelings were returned. Perhaps it *was* better I went as soon and as quietly as possible before things got more complicated.

The only person to discuss this with was Aunt Siobhan, but I'd have to corner her alone which wasn't as easy as it sounded. There were a lot of people in that house and they came and went all day. Eventually, I managed to mouth to her as I was drying the pots she was washing after breakfast, that I needed a quiet word. I'd to be careful as old big-ears Rosie was putting the plates away in the cupboard.

Apart from Rosie there were only Ronan and Molly left in the house, so Siobhan slapped Ronan's drum in his hand and told him to go practice in the barn. By the speed at which he left, I deduced this was not an unwelcome thing. Molly could be packed off anywhere with a book - within five minutes she'd be in another country. And Rosie?

"Rosie, go pick some strawberries - I'll be making meringue tomorrow. Only good ones mind. No-one wants to find half a slug on their spoon - they'll be wondering where the other half went."

Very nicely done, I thought.

That left the two of us until Craig hurried in looking for a halter for moving a bull, which his dad had left behind the coal bucket next to the hearth. Siobhan picked it up, threw it at him and told him to *"gread leat"*, which was close enough to 'get lost' for me to understand.

My aunt put a steaming pot of tea before me and said quietly:

"What's so important you want your Da and brothers and sisters out of the way?"

I explained what I had been thinking about, especially the bit about Aidan and the fondness growing between us, although I blushed furiously. She put her hand on my cheek.

"I understand – truly I do. But don't you think leaving in secret might have the opposite effect on Aidan than the one you intend? Folks hereabouts have known him all his life and will soon come to terms with the happenings in their village. It would be different for you. Why don't you ask Daniel – he's his friend."

"He told me to ask you."

"*Maith do*", whispered Auntie tight-lipped, and at my incomprehension, "Good of him."

The following week Aidan called at our farm, to see Danny. His father's horse was tied up in the yard and although I'd avoided facing facts, this conversation couldn't be put off any longer.

I spent a few minutes in my room, combing through and plaiting my hair and tidying my appearance.

Dan wasn't exactly subtle – as soon as I walked in, he walked out, and left Aidan and me staring awkwardly at each other. He coughed and loosened his collar. For some goddamn reason I curtseyed. Which made him laugh and that broke the ice.

"We need to speak, Lorelei," he said, running a strand of my hair between his fingers. It's true you must go, but it won't be forever."

That took away the responsibility I had been dreading. He'd broached the subject first.

I replied with more confidence than I felt:

"We'll meet up again when things get better."

He nodded but his grip on my hand tightened and he pulled me into a hug.

"I know you must go, Lorelei darlin' but my heart aches so for your loss," he said, and he kissed me.

I studied his face to imprint it in my mind. It was a strong face, but with a sadness about his expressive mouth. I wanted him to kiss me again.

He did, longer, harder and with more passion than before, so it was probably as well Rosheen took that moment to come looking for garden twine. Aidan's 'tut' was clearly audible, so she backed out at the double.

"I know we're still too young for anything more permanent, but this will keep you safe on your travels - think of me often. He took a little case from his riding jacket pocket and squeezed it into my hand.

"Perhaps one day I'll be able to exchange it for a wedding band."

Inside was a very pretty gold cross on a chain - I'd never had so fine a gift. Incised on the back was 'Lorelei'. It brought tears to my eyes. I could so easily love this boy.

"I'll be proud to wear it, Aidan Valentine," I said, suddenly shy. "Will you clasp it for me?"

He did, and held me to his chest for a moment, the tweed of his jacket rough against my cheek. Then he was gone, riding down the lane and out of my life.

I watched him go and suddenly my sister Rosheen was beside me, kissing my cheek in comfort, her arm about my shoulders.

Chapter Eleven
Heartbreak and Violence

The day I left, I watched the dawn break opalescent above the dark green hills and thought my heart would break.

One by one the birds began to trill, until the air fairly rang.

A tiny ant tickled its way across my hand, and I gently laid it down with its battalion to carry a severed leaf to its lair. It would stay, and I must go.

Back to the dirt and despondency of city life; back to broken people and soot-encrusted bricks; back to lads with Brylcreem and flick-knives - a world away from my Daniel with love for all God's creation in his shining eyes.

What had auntie called me? 'A ragged little skeleton with a white face.' Would I become that again..... *could* I become that again?

The bane of my life, my pretty little curly-haired Rosie, came quiet for once, and laid her head in my lap. Her shoulders heaved, and I felt her warm tears through the cotton of my skirt.

One by one my cousins all arrived with a small gift – a copy of Gatsby in a leather cover from Molly; a wooden flute Ronan had carved himself from a sycamore branch, a yard of satin ribbon from Rosheen – each gift small and personal to its giver.

My leaving in some respects was a replay of my arrival.

My cousins stood in line, each one scrubbed and in their Sunday best. Daniel, Rosheen, Molly, Sean, Ronan, Craig, and last but by no means least, Rosie – all standing like soldiers on parade. I kissed and hugged them all. Little Rosie put her arms round my neck and whimpered against my shoulder.

I knelt down and whispered in her ear:

"I need someone to take care of Gealach for me while I'm away. She'll need feeding, grooming and exercise and her tack will need looking after. She's a living creature – you won't be able to skip your responsibility if it's snowing, or if you just don't feel like getting out of bed. Do you think you could do that? If I'm not back in a year she's yours. But you must ask Da first – she had been his gift to me."

She stood back, filled her lungs and bellowed:

"Da – Bridie says I can have Gealach. Can I?"

"That's not quite what I said!"

I reiterated the conversation to Conn who understood completely:

"She's been told she can't offload Gealach onto someone else. She's her responsibility and if I'm not back within the year, she'll be hers to keep. I can't just leave Gealach uncared for, and I'm sure my littlest sister is old enough to understand that," I explained to my uncle, ruffling Rosie's curls.

She nodded enthusiastically.

"Please Da…., *please,*" said Rosie, totally overdoing it.

"You'll be held to account daughter. I'll countenance no cruelty to animals on this farm."

Rosie's head rocked as if on a spring.

Aunt Siobhan came fussing out of the house with a wicker basket of food for the journey, just in time to hear the end of the exchange.

"Cruelty? There'll be no cruelty to animals while I draw breath on this farm!"

The kids rolled their eyes in unison.

Auntie hugged me so tightly I thought I'd suffocate, then ran back inside sobbing as if her heart would break. One of her chicks was leaving the nest.

Uncle Conn himself was to drive me to Dublin, and at the last minute Daniel managed to bully Craig into watching the horses and leapt aboard the dog-cart beside his father.

I sat disconsolate in the back with my baggage. I was going with more style than I arrived, and with infinitely more heartbreak.

We reached the port of Dublin far faster than I would have liked. Daniel, doing his best to keep my spirits up, picked me up by the waist from the rear of the dogcart and swung me down onto my feet, catching my new skirt on one of the cart's iron hinges and ripping a hole in the hem.

Uncle took the suitcase Aunt Siobhan had carefully packed for me and checked it in with the shipping company. It was far grander than the carpet bag I'd arrive with and had a leather label for my destination and address. This had caused something of a problem. I was going to New York, but where? I'd had no contact with my family since I'd left.

After much discussion it was decided to pay for storage in the shipping office at New York, until I could sort out a place to stay.

I was scared. New York where I'd been born was now as foreign to me as the far side of the moon. Although I supposed my O'Neill aunts and uncle would acknowledge me, I had no confidence they'd take me in. They'd shown little to no interest in me since I left and my mother was probably singing 'When Oirish Oiz are Smilin'' for pennies on a street corner by now.

As we waited, my terror increased, until I was thinking seriously of buying a gun and taking on the whole village of Cordonagh single-handed.

On the other hand, I had absolute confidence in my Cullen family. Auntie Siobhan wouldn't let a little thing like the Atlantic come between her and one of her chicks in trouble.

The liner was already docked when we arrived and final supplies were being loaded. The quay was crowded with people like us, all in their best clothes. Some of the ladies carried vanity cases and wore cloche hats, and the gentlemen had suits with baggy pants and tie-pins and cuff-links.

Uncle had tucked my ticket and passport into my purse before we'd left Long Barrow.

I was to travel third-class, which while not luxurious, was a world away from Dungannon Road.

There wasn't much conversation – pleasantries seemed out of place. I took hold of Daniel and Uncle Conn by the hand and held on tight like a frightened child. I saw them glance at each other over my head.

There was a shout and a loud crack.

The crowd turned as one, then the passengers nearest the bow ran in panic, bumping into others on their way. A fight had broken out amongst half a dozen stevedores and one of them had pulled a gun.

One man was lying motionless on the ground and the others backed away in a semi-circle in terror. A young boy at the end of the line of fighters turned to run and got a bullet in the leg. He screamed and fell. I saw the blood oozing between his fingers.

The newly formed and inexperienced Garda police dashed the length of the liner to the scene, and before anyone could act, the perpetrator put the gun in his mouth and pulled the trigger. Blood sprayed up the side of the ship and covered the concrete quay. Those passengers who had been slow getting out of the way found themselves splattered with gore.

Dan grabbed me and threw me halfway across the dock out of harm's way. I skidded over the concrete which tore lumps out of my shins and skinned my elbows and cheek.

Uncle, grim faced, pushed Danny behind him and I could see in his mind he was back fighting the English in the days before I'd arrived. It was a terrible thing to see a man so conditioned to danger. I hardly recognized the kind and indulgent uncle I knew.

The Garda had covered the man who had been killed, had the other culprits in handcuffs and were marching them away. One of the passengers took off his Mackintosh and placed it over the decapitated body on the ground.

Daniel gently took his father by the arm, and I saw the light of reality gradually return to Uncle Conn's eyes. He shook his head as if he'd awoken from dreams – which I suppose in a way he had.

Then he did something else quite unexpected. He grabbed my purse from my hand and strode across the concrete quay, disappearing from sight behind the prow of the liner.

"No idea," Daniel said at my questioning look. "We can't move away or he'll never find us in this crowd."

But the crush was getting smaller as the first-class passengers had started boarding. There were hundreds of people waiting to embark, taken by travel class, so I was quite far down on the list.

An ambulance, bell ringing, came and removed the bodies seemingly abandoned on the quay, and helped the boy with the gunshot wound into the back – all three – living and dead - lumped together in an untidy pile of arms and legs.

"Catholics and Protestants, I guess. Is there no end to it?" muttered Dan.

I was now getting in a panic myself – not because of the time, but because uncle had taken my purse which contained my travel documents, passport and money.

Dan kept craning his neck trying to locate his father, but he wasn't tall enough to see over the throng.

"Don't worry," he said, more to rally himself than me I suspected. "He'll be back in a few minutes – you know Da."

I did, but it was still a relief when he found us an hour later. He was clutching my purse and a wad of papers, and pushing none too politely through the hordes of people still cluttering the ends of the gangplanks.

Uncle Conn dragged us away and stood with his back to the ship. He sorted his papers into order.

"Tickets – one for you too, son – I'm not putting our girl in danger. You're to go with her. Take out your pocketbook."

He handed Daniel the two tickets, my passport and notarized identification documents to allow Danny emergency passage. There was also a fat manilla envelope which he was instructed not to open until he reached the privacy of the cabin.

"Fortunately, Bridie's papers are made out in the name of Cullen, so I was able to book you in as newlyweds. You can share a cabin."

He lowered his head until he was staring his oldest son in the eyes.

"And I expect you to behave like a gentleman Daniel Cullen – do you understand me?"

Daniel was red in the face with mortification. After all I was his sister of sorts, but he stood tall, proud of his new responsibility.

We'd to run after Uncle Conn, because as soon as all this was concluded, he made a bee-line for the gates, overcome with emotion. Then he hugged the son who'd never been further away from home than Dublin, and his newly-acquired daughter, who could be returning to the penury she came from. Kissing us both and not confident he'd see either of us again, he left.

Dan and I felt like 'babes in the wood'. I just hoped I didn't look as lost as he did.

Chapter Twelve
Back to the Beginning

Our cabin was about as big as my old home in Dungannon Road, but although only third class, it was decidedly more luxurious. Our ship had been pretty much knocked together from an old cargo boat, the sumptuous cruise liners having been taken for troop carriers in the Great War and mostly now laying at the bottom of the Atlantic.

Even so, I was gratified to see that for me there would be a soft bed, though poor Danny would be relegated to the floor.

It was a deathly boring ten days of choppy grey ocean to the horizon. We saw an iceberg – a long way off thankfully.

Apart from that, there were only two other happenings of note.

When we opened Uncle Conn's envelope, it held a breath-taking five hundred English pounds – three hundred in twenty-pound notes and the rest in smaller denominations.

And the second occurrence, probably more important as far as I was concerned, I caught a glimpse of Clara Bow on the First-Class Promenade deck. I vowed always to wear fox furs and buckles on my shoes.

The money allowed Daniel to fit himself out with new clothes from the onboard shops. He looked very dapper in navy serge with a high starched collar and silk tie. They complimented his auburn curls, which much to my displeasure he had the shipboard barber trim. His green Irish eyes twinkled with delight as he examined himself in the mirror.

"My Mam wouldn't know me. Eat your heart out Douglas Fairbanks!"

At journey's end, we disembarked in a cacophony of instructions, immigration officials, queues and jostling. First class passengers, naturally, bypassed immigration procedures. I caught a quick glance of Clara's airy hairdo as she ducked into her limousine on the enormous concourse.

Dan had shoved our money in his underwear for safety. Just the thought of where it'd been inclined me to thrift.

We checked on my luggage then took a cab to Pennsylvania Station. It wasn't far and seemed a good place to start looking for a hotel. A HOTEL! I'd never been across the steps of one in all my life.

The closest to the station was, aptly, the Pennsylvania, but the receptionist took one look at us and called security. We were unceremoniously put out on our ear. I looked Danny up and down – he didn't appear *that* disreputable. It took a while for the penny to drop – no wedding ring. They thought I was a floozy.

Once we'd put that right, we found respectable accommodation in a small hotel in a side-street in Chelsea, a mile from the station. We ate in a nearby coffee house then slept for ten hours straight.

So... what next? I'd crossed the ocean – twice – the second time toting my poor bemused cousin who was even less experienced than me. The one thing in our favor was that we were solvent, and thanks to the generosity of Uncle Conn, if we were careful, we would remain so for quite a while.

It was to our advantage as it turned out, that we'd been ejected from the smart hotel. The owner of the small one we eventually chose, being romantically inclined, decided we as newlyweds should be shown just how hospitable the people of the city of New York could be – especially if your name was Cullen and your landlady's husband was a Callaghan of County Cork.

Mrs. Callaghan arranged for her brother-in-law to haul my belongings from the station and stored them in her washroom in the hotel cellar. When I wept with relief she fished a creased linen hankie out of the wash-basket and handed it to me to blow my nose.

Dan still looked despondent. Apart from the annual trip to Dublin with his father, his only other experience of city life was watching a member of the IRA spread the inside of his head over the bow of an ocean liner – not exactly a confidence booster.

One grey day I told Danny to put on his oldest clothes for a visit to my former family home on Dungannon Road. I ripped a button from his jacket and pulled the hem down on a trouser leg.

We walked the forty minutes to Dungannon Road, my stomach becoming queasier with every step. It wasn't four years since I'd left, so little had changed – except me. I began to see things which must always have been there but I'd never noticed: paint peeling off window frames, overflowing garbage, rusty stair rails and the overwhelming stench of poverty.

There were grubby kids playing in the street - just as I had with poor Jimmy Dobson, and my sisters and brothers. Some boys, arses hanging out of their pants, were swinging from the lamp posts; little girls with tangled ringlets and snotty noses played hopscotch on the sidewalks.

Older boys with greased-back hair played with flick-knives and laughing, threatened passers-by from tenement steps.

Prohibition was in full swing or I guessed there'd have been broken glass in the gutters and the stink of stale beer, but the Shamrock where Mr. Kelly had pulled pints and filled jugs for the likes of the O'Neills, was now a junk shop, with dented dolly tubs and possers, chipped pottery and old Victorian cross-stitch epigrams in broken frames, stacked untidily outside. A ragged man with patched work-pants leaned against the wall puffing on a cigarette.

I could see Danny was horrified.

"You lived *here*?" he shuddered.

I confess I was shocked myself.

"Well, hell'll freeze over before I leave you here on your own. Da was right. I did need to come."

"I grew up here Dan. I dare say I'd have managed."

He glared at me.

"Is there anything or anyone you especially want to see? I'll be out of here in an hour and you'll be with me, make no mistake."

We walked halfway down the road and I turned to look at the better of our two homes – the one with running water. It still had our lace curtains but they were dirty and hung down at one side. Mam was a lot of things but a slattern she wasn't, so I knew there were new tenants.

A young man was leaning against the door jamb opposite. He was pale and thin, like a plant that's been left to grow in the dark, and his trouser legs and shirt sleeves were six inches too short, as if he'd shot up overnight. He was wearing an old knitted vest which was fraying at the hem. He seemed familiar - he was staring back at me too. The penny dropped for us both at the same moment. It was Morgan Allen who used to wolf-whistle at me.

He made as if to cross the street, then turned on his heel and sauntered down the road whistling. Dan…. he'd turned away because of Dan. I couldn't say I was sorry – he always was a dumbass.

We braved cat-calls from the neighborhood bullies and walked into Dean Street, and there was Burt Greenwood's hardware store, neat and shiny as a new pin, as it always had been.

Also neat and shiny was Lilian Greenwood with a gold band on the third finger of her left hand, and her blouse buttoned up to her chin. She was arranging screw-drivers in a display in the window, helped by a serious-looking young man in spectacles who turned and kissed her cheek. Old Burt was sitting on a folding stool in the doorway smoking a cigarette. Only four years? Well, who'd have thought it? Michael'd be spinning in his grave.

I found I didn't want to speak to her either. She was like a specter from another time and place.

"Just one more call, please." I said to Daniel. "Then we can leave."

I decided to visit my Aunt Dolly's. That was the only place big enough to take more than her and Uncle Sam, so if my sister and brother were anywhere, it would be there. It was a very tidy little terraced house with a tiny enclosed front garden only large enough for a single tea-bush, its scent overpowering in the enclosed space.

Uncle Sam opened the door, customary copy of the New York Times in his hand. He hadn't changed – sandy comb-over and wire-rimmed spectacles perched halfway down his nose.

I introduced Daniel and asked if Auntie Dolly was home.

"You're lucky," he said without enthusiasm. "The other two are here as well."

Kitty's face appeared over his shoulder. She'd blossomed somewhat – grown a chest and   had hair almost as light as my own. She knocked Uncle Sam face-first into the door and hugged me, jiggling me round as if we'd actually liked each other at some point.

"Bill," she yelled, "come see who's here!"

My brother had been 'Billy' when I left but he must be twelve now so things may have change. He hadn't though – skin smooth as a girls and skinned knees.

"Oh hi, Bridie – who's that?" he said as if I'd left yesterday. I pulled a reluctant Daniel forward.

"This is your cousin Daniel. Daniel Cullen," I added the last by way of explanation when their faces turned blank. "You know – from Ireland… Mam's brother's son…. where I went when I left here."

Darn but they were dumb.

At that moment Auntie Dolly arrived. She pushed her husband and my brother and sister up the hall, taking charge.

"Well, what're you standing there for? Fetch the young man inside. I dare say some tea would go down well," she said, beaming at Danny who did his best to smile back.

Over cups of tea I was given their news.

"Rosie died of the DTs last Fall," said Uncle Sam, not able to repress his relief.

"And Lily married the Protestant vicar's son Matty Dawson. He's a meathead, forever mooning over her, in front of everyone, too," added Billy.

Aunt Dolly gave him a smack round the ear for being cheeky in front of Dan. I wished she'd seen my cousin deck Aidan at the dance.

Kitty was still working at the mill. Billy took great delight in telling me, although she was knocking on, no-one had offered for her yet. Knocking on? She can't have been more than seventeen.

In retaliation, Kitty added that Bill couldn't read or write and had been known to run messages for Mr. Luciano.

Although Auntie had steam coming out of her ears at the mere mention of the hoodlum's name, Uncle seemed glad of a few extra bucks, and looked down at the Times to hide his smirk.

I told them about Ireland and the dreadful sectarian fighting. Daniel described its beauty and the horses his father had made his sole responsibility. His face lit up with pride as he said it.

Auntie told me the weight-gain looked good on me – just what every girl wants to hear. She also said my hair looked very pretty but my skin was too brown. I should wear a hat outdoors.

I could just imagine me in a hat feeing the pigs and mucking out the cows. I could see Daniel was having the same thought. He coughed into his handkerchief.

I kissed everyone on the cheek and Aunt Dolly and Kitty kissed Daniel. We turned to wave as we walked down the path, but Auntie had already closed the door. I knew with as much clarity as I'd had the day I'd left Mam, I'd never set eyes on them again.

Our next consideration was to find some way to survive – Uncle Conn's generous gift wouldn't last forever.

We stayed on at Mrs. Callaghan's while Dan suffered a dismal year of flipping burgers – he looked ridiculous in a silly paper hat – and selling newspapers on street corners. He finally landed a job at Belmont Racetrack at Elmont just outside the city limits.

It was only mucking out the stables at first, but as long as he was with horses he was happy.

It was inevitable that before long his talents would become noticed.

He had learned much from his father, and once when Uncle Conn had been detained in Dublin by a snowstorm, I'd watched Dan deliver a foal with such delicacy and calm I'd been amazed. It was a privilege to see that beautiful baby, scrubbed down with straw by my cousin, learn to control its wobbly legs and take its first taste of its mother's milk.

Dan also knew how to ease and bind sprains and treat bruising, how to calm a creature in pain.

So, although Daniel had no formal training, it didn't take long for the breeders and their head grooms and veterinarians to understand his worth. He was gradually absorbed into the day to day care of the horses, and by stages he was allowed to exercise them, increasing their speed to a canter, then a short gallop.

He avoided the breeders when he could – they were a combination of hardnosed businessmen and flamboyant entrepreneurs. Their wives had big-brimmed hats and wore footwear more appropriate to a Hollywood film set.

I had one or two jobs in stores but hated the turned-up noses of the supervisors, and when one of them picked on a little junior and made her cry, I stamped on the woman's foot, yelled a rude word in her face and got fired.

Eventually, as Dan's star rose, it took mine along with it.

I started as a stable-hand, interspersed with helping Daniel with his doctoring when required. My employment didn't pay much, but we were able to move our belongings from Mrs. Callaghan's to a tiny apartment near the racecourse.

We did okay. We'd plenty to eat and a warm place to sleep at night, but with two of us in a confined space there was little social life other than by prior arrangement.

One or two guys took me out to the picture house but once they realized there would be no 'canoodling on the back porch', they lost interest pretty quickly.

Dan wasn't bothered. Girls flirted with him all the time, but he was far more interested in his horses.

Reduced circumstances meant we spent many hours indulging in the free entertainment New York afforded. I became quite an expert on the painter Kandinsky through sitting in the warmth of countless galleries.

Occasionally, Danny and I would visit a picture palace together and marvel at the movies where everyone mimed with the sound turned off. I looked forward to the day, if it ever came, when Rudolph Valentino told the heroine he loved her instead of flinging his arms all over and nearly knocking her on her ass.

Chapter Thirteen
Kidnapped

One day our exploration took us to what must have been one of the most depressing parts of New York – 11th Avenue, close to the docks and bordering 'Hell's Kitchen'.

The streets and warehouses nearby were always dank and the sun rarely penetrated the gloom.

We skipped on and off the uneven sidewalks like children, munching on now-squashed sandwiches Mrs. Callaghan had been good enough to pack into a paper bag.

On the wall of an abandoned warehouse a tattered handbill was slapped haphazardly on the grimy brickwork.

June 8th – Belmont Stakes

Dan's stopped in his tracks:

"How in God's Holy Name could I have let that pass me by? One of the most important races of the year and where I work, too!"

"Too much time with your head up a horses ass?" I said wryly. "I take it we'll be there?"

"I'll be worked off my feet – worked harder than I ever did in my whole life, darn it!" he said, looking delighted.

We resumed our saunter along the road, oblivious to all around us, laughing and making plans for June 8th

Uncle Conn raised standardbred horses which were mostly for harness racing and were stockier than thoroughbreds. Belmont was a flat course for the latter.

Daniel suddenly lurched into the gutter away from me and fell awkwardly to his knees, hit in the hamstrings by a tall ungainly fellow with large yellow teeth and outstandingly long legs,

"You'll be excusing me, young Sir and yourself Miss O'Neill. I've to take you to see the master, Mr. Cathal O'Neill himself," he said in an Irish accent the like of which I'd never heard. He hoisted Dan by the coat collar and set him on his feet again.

"Follow this way, if you please," and rather than following, he pushed us down a side alley.

It's a strange thing about New York – you can skip down an alleyway from one street to another and be in an entirely different world.

The difference this time was an affluent street of shops with apartments above, and a clean busy feel about it. Ladies in cloche hats carried beautifully wrapped packages to luxurious automobiles. It was difficult to imagine the same city could contain Dungannon Road.

I stood up tall and stuck my nose in the air.

"And who in the name of God and All his Saints is Cathal O'Neill?

Dan, having been on the receiving end of this creature's ministrations already, could see himself having to defend me and paled. Daniel was a lover not a fighter – despite his run-in with Aidan, again on my behalf.

"Mr. O'Neill is Himself O'Neill, Chief of the Donegal O'Neill's – the original family you'll know. Not all left with Lord Hugh in seven.

"That'll be 1607," said a sardonic voice behind me. "On your way, Domnall."

Our apprehender tugged his forelock and sloped off.

Chapter Fourteen
Cathal O'Neill (Himself) Esq.

I directed my attention to the speaker and got a surprise. As I turned, my nose almost collided with his chest – he must have been close on six feet and a half.

Looking up, I drew myself to my full height – all five feet four of it - and addressed him:

"To what end are we to be detained Mr. O'Neill? I take it that's who you are?"

"Indeed it is," he said smiling down at me.

He had very even, very white teeth. The rest of his face, from my viewpoint silhouetted against a bright blue sky, was still unclear.

"Now, I'd be much obliged if you'd join me for a dish of tea – or something stronger?" the gentleman said to Dan.

A glass of grog would have gone down well with me too, given that I was about to be abducted against my will.

"No Sir. I shall remain on this public street until you explain yourself," I said stoutly, although Mr. O'Neill didn't seem even remotely interested.

I took a couple of steps back so I could at least look him in the eye – and what an eyeful he was!

He had a kind, humorous face – in my limited experience unusual in a man so handsome. His hair was colored like my own but slightly darker and more vibrant. It had a natural unruly curl which was most attractive I thought.

Dan kicked my ankle to remind me staring was rude.

"Now if you'll come away with me we'll visit my sister where we can talk privately," he continued his conversation with Daniel. "It's yourself, Mr. Cullen, I have business with rather than this delightful young lady.

"It concerns horses which I believe are your specialty. And tell me, aren't your family from County Wicklow?" he asked conversationally. Now just how in God's name did he know that?

The mention of horses immediately engaged Danny's attention and when Mr. O'Neill began to stride up the street, Dan ran and caught him up.

He and Mr. 'Himself' strode up the street together, Dan occasionally adding a skips-step to keep up, and I suppressed a giggle at the sight of them chatting away, my cousin with his head tipped back to hear.

I was brought back to reality once I remembered Dan was such an innocent, but no-one was taking a blind bit of notice of anything I said. I'd have to go along with them although it seemed I was surplus to requirements.

We crossed the road to a little private park with trailing willows along a small artificial water complex.

On the other side was a row of immaculate brownstone residences with flights of steps to arched doorways.

They were enormous – taller than our tenements, some of which housed ten families.

Mr. O'Neill rapped at a door with a number '18' of polish brass between two stained glass panels.

The door was opened by a lady in a drop-waisted dress. She wore a fashionable blonde bob and had a pretty dimpled smile.

"Come on in, Cathal my darlin' – and a welcome to your guests."

She smiled at us both individually and we were immediately captivated.

"This is my sister Neave," Cathal O'Neill introduced us. "Neave, this is Daniel Cullen, son of Colin Cullen who raises the finest trotters in Ireland, and his cousin Bridie, also an O'Neill."

He clapped Daniel on the back.

"Come, lad…let's have that whisky."

"Jonathan's waiting in your study, dear. He's due at Belmont tomorrow and just dropped in with a question or two."

"That's Jon Grainger, my business manager. Come, I'll introduce you."

The two of them strolled out of the hall through a half-open door to the right, which shut behind them. I was left standing awkwardly next to Neave O'Neill to whom so far I'd spoken not one word.

"Come along, Bridie – we'll have our own little party. You wouldn't want to be there in any case. Cathal is the very definition of tedium when he gets on about horses. Jonathan's the same," smiled Neave.

"Dan's as bad. He has six brothers and sisters and they can all wear out their tongues on their own subjects – Dan's just happens to be horses. But then so is his father's, their next-door neighbor's and his son, who is Dan's friend."

"And so what's *your* passion, Bridie?" asked Neave and to a hovering maid, "Tea in the sitting room, Martha. Unless you'd prefer something else?" she asked me.

I said tea would be fine.

We entered a room the like of which I'd only seen in newspaper advertisements for smart hotels.

It had an enormous chandelier with rainbow droplets, a thick circular rug in blue and cream, and a white marble fireplace, fluted in the modern style.

The ceiling must have been twenty feet high, and tall sash windows, shutters stowed, covered the whole of one wall.

I pulled myself together trying my best not to stare and considered Neave's question. Did I have a passion? I did but I doubt most people would have recognized it as such. Neave was awaiting my answer, head on one side:

"I don't know if you'd call it a passion…." I began shyly.

I was terrified of my next admission to such a fine lady.

"I grew up in Irish New York. My father could only get piece work so we'd no regular money coming in until my sister Kitty got a place at a mill…"

I shut up sharp. I was telling this stranger – this rich as Croesus stranger - my dissolute life story.

"There were one or two family problems and I ended up in Ireland staying with my mother's brother and his family in County Wicklow," I said, giving her the short version.

Although my 'passion' was yet to be admitted, that'd do for now. I prayed Miss O'Neill would leave it at that.

"My own background could be considered questionable too," said Neave O'Neill thoughtfully.

This was a well-spoken, fashionable, educated young woman - what could she possibly have in common with me?

"It's true. Our branch of the family was one of those left behind when O'Neill of Tyrone fled to Spain in 1607. -we Irish-born O'Neills have long memories," she chuckled.

"The recent Troubles persuaded us to buy this little bolt-hole and Cathal relocated most of his business to the United States. Our ancestral home in Ireland stands right on the border between the north and south, which can make it very uncomfortable at times.

Her face fell and she changed tack.

"If you please, do go on with your own story."

No chance of the shortened version going unchallenged.

"My brothers and sisters and I pretty much dragged ourselves up. When my brother Mick died of the Spanish Influenza after the war and my Pa hung himself from the tenement rafters, my Mam took to the drink and packed me off to County Wicklow."

Oh my Lord, she was looking at me as if my head had fallen off and rolled across the floor.

"But you're a charming young lady. How can this be so?"

I know she didn't mean to be patronizing but that's how it sounded to me. I straightened my shoulders.

"That can be put at the door of my Aunt Siobhan, Danny's mother. She took me in as one of her own. She clothed me and the whole family gave me much more than just book-learning. They gave me a home and a life."

Dan and Mr. Cathal interrupted our discussion which was perhaps as well. It was beginning to get over-emotional.

"Bridie O'Neill - no relation - may I introduce Jonathan Grainger, who takes care of business for me here in America."

"Charmed, my lady.." he said kissing my hand, his eyes crinkling at the corners.

Jonathan Grainger didn't have Cathal's height but his dark hair and piercing blue eyes were immediately arresting. He'd only spoken one sentence to me, but already I knew he was a flirt and a lady's man.

"Daniel tells me he has an interest in the rearing of thoroughbreds," said Cathal to Jonathan.

Now wasn't that just the understatement of the century!

"He also, quite innocently, happened to drop the name 'Niall Valentine' into the conversation. You may not know it Miss O'Neill, but Mr. Niall Valentine is the foremost breeder of thoroughbreds in Ireland – possibly in the world since Irish blood-lines are without doubt the best."

"Yes indeed. Mr. Valentine has a knowledge of horses unmatched here in the United States," explained Mr. Grainger.

His accent wasn't New York - I'd guess at Kentucky given his profession - certainly somewhere further south.

"Please excuse me, Misses O'Neill and you, young sir. I must be about my business." Then to Cathal. "Sedgewick's pretty much in the bag but I've yet to see Colonel Thomas. I'll keep in touch."

He strode out of the room, straight backed and confident and a moment later the door slammed shut.

"Miss O'Neill is from here in New York, Cathal," said Neave. "I was telling her something of our branch of the O'Neills. I don't believe we have a family connection. It's hard to be sure though," she said smiling at me over the rim of her teacup.

"For all our fine airs and graces," she waved her hand to encompass the room, "it shouldn't be forgotten our grandfather was little more than a gypsy, moving from place to place, fair to fair, buying and selling animals and training his sons and grandsons – including Cathal - to harness race through the streets of market towns," Neave explained. "These were rough people. I saw several accidents as a child – It would shock you to know what."

Dungannon Road where it wasn't unknown for children to fall under the wheels of a rag and bone cart, may have come as something of a surprise to Miss O'Neill.

"But our grandfather Seamus was canny with money and saved every penny he earned trading and betting his horses."

Cathal took up the story.

"Seamus and his three brothers had the same knack for business. These were no folks for hiding their earnings in their socks.

"The youngest – Brian – in particular became adept at playing the money markets and over a period of time they used their riches in a passion common to them all – horseflesh.

"You will understand our wealth has often been obtained through trading less than ethically – often illegally. In other words we come from a family of crooks."

I saw Danny's mouth drop open.

"You're not….. you're not THOSE O'Neills? The ones who drove Mr. Valentine's father into bankruptcy then took his whole herd in settlement?"

I thought Dan was about to burst a blood vessel. His face had turned puce and spittle was spraying from his mouth with each word he uttered.

Brother and sister shared an apprehensive glance. I thought Cathal would continue but it was Neave who spoke.

"Please sit down, Daniel and let us expl…."

"The fuck I will!" yelled Dan with enough force to rattle the chandelier on the ceiling above. "And you can take your job and stick it Mr. Cathal O'Neill, God damn you to hell!"

He strode out of the room in fury.

There was a loud bang, the door reopened and Cathal O'Neill's lackey Domnall emerged dangling a speechless Dan by his shirt collar.

"And what will I be doing with this one, Sir?" he asked, as a devastated Daniel wriggled from his grasp.

Cathal rubbed his face with his palm.

"Let him go," he said.

Chapter Fifteen
Cathal Fails to Explain and Neave Gets Tipsy

I was presented with a conundrum.

Did I stay loyal to my cousin Daniel or indulge my curiosity. After all, I was an O'Neill myself, if not hopefully, 'one of THOSE O'Neills'.

Curiosity won out – I'd find Dan later.

Brother and sister stood together. Both were upset, but it seemed to me Cathal was devastated. So I addressed Neave:

"Is there more or is that the whole Apocalypse?" I asked, using a word I'd last heard in Dean Street Primitive Methodist Church Sunday School.'

"Do you want to know more?" she asked, doubtfully.

"Of course I want to know more. I'm Bridget O'Neill daughter of Robert O'Neill, sister of Michael, Kathleen, Sarah and William O'Neill, niece of Frank O'Neill. I'd sweep that lot under the carpet if I could but the bastards keep popping out again, damn them."

I only stopped there because I'd run out of breath. There was a lot more where that came from.

Cathal sat down and gazed unseeingly out of the window at the busy street and park beyond. He ran a hand aggressively through his hair.

"You will please excuse my language ladies but this bloody family will be the death of me," said Cathal.

And what language was that? I'd heard worse at my Mam's knee.

"If you'll listen Bridget…" he began.

"Bridie," I said.

"Bridie…I'd like to explain what happened. Then I'll help find your cousin if that's what you'd like."

Neave showed her less ladylike side.

"**Marthaaa!** Take away the china and crack open the whisky. Hold the soda. We'll not be needing it."

I regarded her with amazement. She was diminutive, sweet, ladylike and apparently swilled whisky like a docker.

Cathal left, taking his imminent explanation with him.

His sister shrugged.

"No staying power," she said. "I'll save him the trouble. You'll need to know sooner or later.

"Our grandfather stole the Valentine prize herd. No violence you understand, Granddaddy Seamus was too smart to take on the English military.

"He just bought up Edmond Valentine's not-insubstantial debts and took his horses in payment. Big debt – whole herd bar a couple of mares, I think."

Dan was more disturbed than I by this revelation, but I thought horses were beautiful whereas he thought they were worthy of worship.

In an effort to fill the hole left in the conversation by Cathal's departure, I rapidly changed the subject:

"Are you still interested in hearing about 'my passion'? Or have you had enough of obsessions for one day?"

The whisky was starting to make Miss O'Neill giggly.

"Go ahead," she encouraged taking a good pull from her glass.

"My passion is…" *Oh Lord, this was going to sound so pathetic.* "My passion is Ireland – all of it."

I gave it a moment's extra thought.

"Except perhaps some of the people."

"You're not wrong there," agreed my new confidante.

"Ireland is so ancient its very stones whisper to the earth," I said, poetically. Neave coughed.

"Even the rivers and streams have their own music, For me the sun shines brightest there.

"But I love it most when trees break, grey on grey, through a blanket of fog, which clings to the mountains and collects in the valleys and ghosts wail of wrongs gone by."

She was choking on her drink so I slapped her on the back and continued.

"My Cullen family are the very definition of loving kindness. You seem to have had more of a problem."

"Not wrong there either," said Neave putting her shoed feet up on the chair arm and considering her scarlet fingernails.

"Only damn folks on earth who could turn politics into a religion – and a dismal weather outlook into poetry. You sure are passionate!" she chuckled.

I don't know if the laughter was caused by wit or whisky but it served to lighten the mood anyway.

"Time to go find at least one of the fugitives," said Neave slapping the flat of her hand down on her chair arm.. Any thoughts on Daniel's whereabouts? Or shall we start with Cathal? I've a pretty good idea where he is."

Once we'd donned coats and hats we returned to the alley we'd lately been abducted from. It stank of leaky gutters and drains.

"And what would a fine fella like Mr. Cathal be doing down here?"

"Betting on livestock, of course."

Chapter Sixteen
Daniel's Accusation

After Neave with some help from the whisky nearly broke her ankle when her heel caught between two paving slabs, we did eventually track Cathal down.

My initial judgement of Mr. O'Neill as a fine gentleman was about to take a battering.

He was sitting in a basement Speakeasy on Loisaida Avenue shouting at a couple of dubious characters across a table swimming in beer from an over-turned glass. His shirt sleeves were rolled up to the elbows.

As I knew well from my brother Billy, Prohibition was a very hit and miss affair thanks to Mr. Luciano and his cronies. The excise men would close down one joint and it would pop up somewhere else. Didn't seem to matter about jail and fines - the crooks had the authorities in their pockets. You couldn't separate the rich and famous from their cocktails any more than the Irish from their beer.

"…and how would you know anyway, Mr. High-and-Mighty. What does some swell like you know about horseflesh, you arrogant sonofabitch!" the fat man scoffed in broad Brooklynese.

"Because it's an Irish nag, you brainless bastard, and I'm on first name terms with the owner. How else?"

"Ha.. like hell you are, creep. I'd have heard of you if you did… say, who are you anyway?" the man threw in looking a bit less confident.

"I'm Cathal O'Neill. And 'Silver Streak' is a two year old by 'Silver Dollar' out of 'Mamie's Flyer' - my good friend Desmond O'Madden owns the Stud in Tipperary."

Cathal looked his adversary up and down with as much distain as he could muster.

"If I was that eejit I'd keep my gob shut," whispered Neave in my ear. "Next move for Cathal is a fist to the nose and believe me he wouldn't want one of those."

Sadly, the man couldn't hear her and within the minute measured his length on the sawdust of the floor.

"Out! OUT! O U T!" shouted the landlord who had just appeared on the scene. "All of yerz. Yes, you too my fine sir."

Just for a moment, I thought Cathal would flatten him too but Neave was swinging on his arm and dragging him towards the door.

"Come on Cathal O'Neill – lets go home before you get us all locked up and somebody's nag disqualified! You'd melt the Blarney Stone with your lies."

We managed to get him out onto the sidewalk, where he shook us off, still furious.

"I'll kill the bairsted," he fumed, his Irish accent intensifying with his fury.

Once back at the O'Neill house on Byrne Avenue, Cathal flopped into an armchair and removed his shirt collar, still red in the face and perspiring,.

As Neave still looked wobbly on her feet, I went to find her house maid and told her to make lots of strong coffee – and a plate of sandwiches.

I'd no idea what had happened when I'd left the room, but when I returned Neave had gone to sleep curled up in the corner of a plush sofa. Cathal was sitting down at a small writing desk near the window with his head on his folded arms; Dan had come back and was looking mutinous.

"What in the name of all the Angels in Heaven is going on NOW!" I yelled, exasperated.

Martha the maid deposited her tray on a low table and left double-quick.

Cathal heaved himself upright and I couldn't believe the look on his face. This big strong confident man looked completely whipped.

"Ask him," he said, wearily.

"I won't Bridie – so don't even bother asking."

"YOU WON'T WHAT?"

"I won't go back to Ireland with that murderin' bastard!"

"Am I missing something here, Dan? Murdering means there's a dead body. Where is it?"

Daniel spluttered, trying to put together a coherent answer not fueled by temper.

"His grandpa killed Mr. Valentine's father," he said

"So?"

"What do you mean - so?"

"To start with nobody died meaning no-one killed anyone. Whatever happened, took place fifty years ago and - correct me if I'm wrong, Cathal - you were decades away from being born. So what's your problem, Daniel?"

Dan was on the point of tears.

"How could you defend the man whose family did so much harm to Aidan's? You always said you loved Aidan so how could you betray him like this?"

I hoisted him – none too gently – by the arm and made for the door.

"Where are you going?" asked Cathal, confused.

"I'm going to straighten this one out before I resort to murder myself." I scowled. "And don't you go away either."

Chapter Seventeen
Ireland (Again)

Dan and I jumped over the park fence and sat on the grass under a tree. We needed to be that far away from the house for them not to hear what I had to say, although I could see Cathal standing next to the window across the road.

"What in the name of all that's Holy are you thinking, you witless wonder!" I hissed. "What is wrong with you?"

"There's nothing wrong with me – seems the fault is all yours," he glared, shaking my hand from his arm.

"I take it that little chat over the whisky bottle included the offer of a job working with thoroughbreds?"

"A couple with good blood lines - one in particular I've heard of. O'Neill needs a groom - why me? There must be thousands better qualified in America."

Why indeed? But I'd another point to make.

"Have you completely lost your mind? You'd give up your life's ambition to fight a fifty year old battle not even your own? I'm ashamed for you."

Dan's bottom lip was still sticking out but he replied

"Do you suppose I've lost the work for good?"

"If you haven't, you can thank your lucky stars Cathal O'Neill's made of better stuff than his granddaddy – you… you – oh, words fail me! Now get in there and ask his pardon."

Dan did apologize but couldn't look Cathal in the eye for shame.

"I beg your pardon, Mr. O'Neill, for disrespecting your grandfather's name," he muttered.

"Oh, I wouldn't let it bother you," chipped in Neave cheerily. She'd come to and was once again her exhaustingly chirpy self.

"The old bastard deserved everything you thought of him and more besides. That true, Cathal?"

Unbelievably Cathal looked as abashed as Danny.

"Much more, I guess. That's why I wanted you particularly to come back home with me, since you are well known to the Valentine family. I knew your father and Mr. Valentine were business acquaintances" and how did he know that? "but not of their friendship. I have a proposition to put to him, perhaps your father, too. I may count on your discretion?

"I need to know if you'll agree to come back to Ireland, Dan," said Cathal doubtfully, "and help me put things right with Mr. Valentine? Or at least try?"

Daniel nodded, shame-faced but couldn't resist adding.

"For my friend Aidan, you understand."

"Thank the good Lord for that!" said Cathal, slamming an ornately decorated envelope into Daniel's hand and turning back to the window.

I peeped over his shoulder at four First Class tickets for the evening departure of the SS New York sailing three days later.

Neave snatched the tickets from Dan's hand.

"Oh, that's grand! It's an evening departure. We don't have to rush getting ready."

Perhaps I could get out of her how come Cathal knew about the Cullens and the Valentines.

Cathal spent the next couple of days with Jon Grainger, putting his affairs in order. As he proposed being absent for some time, no sales would go ahead until his return and the well-being of his stock would be in the hands of Jonathan and Mr. Razner, his stable master.

A sulky Danny and I spent the time giving in our notice at work and for our apartment and packing our belongings.

Never in my entire life could I have come even close to imagining the luxury of first class liner travel.

Fresh flowers on small tables, plush armchairs, embroidered silk coverlets on the beds. We even had our own private bathroom, Neave and I, and cupboards and wardrobes to spare.

But best of all was a huge sliding window with two deckchairs on a small balcony, where we sat and chatted over cocktails delivered by a uniformed waiter, and Neave smoked cigarettes from an ivory holder. It was here I finally got to ask *the* question:

"Oh," she replied. "My brother had him followed of course. You must have noticed! I wouldn't have thought Domnall was that inconspicuous. He has the longest legs I ever saw and is a thin as a lat!"

I stamped my foot in annoyance as understanding dawned. I'd seen him in a field near 'Redmile' the day Aidan and I rode to Cordonagh, and on Dungannon Road outside the junk shop. There must have been some other occasions I'd never noticed.

Neave fished out the olive and blithely sipped her dry Martini.

The dining room scared the crap out of both Dan and I at first.

The menus were in French which was a decided problem for people who had just about mastered reading English. Although, on second thoughts, if I'd known at the time escargot were snails I probably wouldn't have eaten anything at all for five days. As it was, they were pleasantly chewy things served in shells which were the very devil to eat.

The clientele glittered with diamonds or smoked fat cigars, depending on their sex. I felt at a disadvantaged in a pretty day dress with a lace decolletage and cap sleeves. Of course, this wasn't lost on Neave whose favorite hobby turned out to be shopping – for anyone. A slender young girl made a great mannequin.

Part of the A-deck facilities was a whole street of fancy shops. She dragged me from one end to the other, through every stockist of female attire until we emerged into the sea air on the deck beyond.

I now was the proud possessor of six silk and satin evening gowns in various shades of green and blue - which apparently complimented my red hair - satin shoes with heels and sandals without, an embroidered Spanish shawl, a plethora of stockings and suspenders and – God help us – a mink coat. Once back in the cabin I hung the coat over a wardrobe door and just gazed at it for a full half-hour.

Neave patted my hand and gave me a hankie to mop up the tears seeping down my cheeks.

The following evening I felt far more 'the thing' and even ordered oysters, two of which ended up in my napkin under the table.

I was delighted to see Cathal had outfitted Dan in similar fashion. He looked like a film star in black tie and tuxedo and handsome as the Douglas Fairbanks he had once compared himself to.

It was five full days of utter delight until Ireland loomed large on the horizon and our trunks were packed and stored for disembarkation.

I don't know what I expected from Cathal and Neave's version of Ireland. I doubted it resembled 'Long Barrow' or even the more prestigious Valentine farm at 'Redmile'.

In this, I was entirely right.

Traveling first class we avoided the inconvenience of customs and were collected from the port by the very latest in automobiles with a shiny burgundy body and chrome trim. It was driven by a chauffeur in a kilt.

Once we'd cleared Belfast with its city unpleasantness, we travelled down country lanes lined with ivy-wrapped trees and neatly laid-in ash hedges. The only other vehicle we passed was a large hay-cart which pulled into a field to let us by.

I was fascinated to take in a part of Ireland I was unfamiliar with.

It was very unlike Wicklow and was much given to bogs and loughs lined with clumps of reeds with cotton tops. I got the impression it never completely dried out.

"Horrid, isn't it?" said Neave. "Wait 'til you see where we live. You'll understand why I like New York."

She reverted to gazing out of the window, humming a slightly out of tune version of a song all the rage in New York's less reputable clubs.

Chapter Eighteen
'Túr Capaill'

Cathal was quiet but I got the feeling he was agitated.

"You'd better tell them about Brian," he muttered to his sister, then returned his attention to the passing fields.

"Ah yes… Brian. Hmmm!"

I was agog and I saw Danny lean over to hear too.

"Brian's the last of the disreputable O'Neills. Daddio – sorry can't resist it…."

"The Irish for grandpa," explained Daniel, "is *Daideo*."

"…. Seamus's youngest brother," continued Neave. "He's mad as a hatter but absolutely loaded – mostly with ill-gotten gains."

"Brian's grasp on reality is somewhat tenuous at times," said Cathal, "so we maintain the fiction he's in charge of 'Túr Capaill' to keep him quiet - sorry, happy. He's the last of Seamus's generation, Many of the older clansmen still cling to the memory of the brothers – they consider those the glory days of the O'Neills.

"It makes things awkward at times – especially when he's not exactly lucid. Thankfully, he's topped eighty but it'd be just like him to reach his full century."

"'Túr Capaill'?" I asked.

"With the family's penchant for the obvious, 'Horses Tower' – isn't that just swell?" said Neave, wrapping her blanket more tightly round her knees, "I haven't named the New York house yet but I'm open to suggestions.

Something like 'Swing-time' or 'Carolina Moon' would be just fine."

When we'd bumped and swerved our way across what seemed like the whole of Ireland we reached the new border just south of Strabane where a grim-looking guard stood at the bridge of a river crossing.

When he recognized the car, he stood aside and waved us through. Cathal nodded to him as we passed.

"It's his job to stop traffic across the new border at this point but he's a Tyrone O'Neill," said Cathal.

From this point on, the dreadful roads became truly abysmal and at one point Cathal had to take the wheel while Daniel and a red-faced chauffeur, apparently swearing profusely in Irish, heaved one of the rear wheels out of a pothole. As Cathal put his foot on the gas, Neave knelt on the back seat and howled with laughter as Dan and the chauffeur were both sprayed head to foot in muddy water.

It was fortunate we arrived at 'Túr Capaill' within the half-hour because Dan was shaking like a leaf from the cold, even though Neave had wrapped him in her blanket.

The drive to the house was the best bit of road we'd hit since we'd left Belfast, and as we rounded a bend the Tower came into full view.

My first impression was it had more in common with Transylvania than an Irish country manor.

It's façade was composed of corner towers with the house wall between.

The ruined upper stories had empty windows, silhouetted against a watery sunset. The center wall comprised a row of arches and a door which wouldn't have looked out of place on a castle. Next to it was a Gothic bell-pull with a metal handle.

As we stepped from the car I caught a glance of Neave looking ruefully at her brother before clapping her hands and saying in an appalling American accent:

"Come on y'all!"

Cathal trailed behind, hands in pockets, gazing down at the gravel beneath his feet. He looked sad but quickened his pace to enter first as a maid opened the door.

"Good day to you, Sir. Good day, Miss Neave. And the welcome of 'Túr Capaill' to the lady and gentleman," she trotted out.

"You'll be wanting to clean up a bit and rest.

"Cara – Mr. Cullen to the Chevalier room," Neave looked at me and groaned. "Miss Bridget to the Narraghmore room – Derby winner 1891. Bits of Seamus linger on thanks to Uncle Brian."

"Domnall has put your luggage in your rooms. An hour and a half do? I'll arrange dinner for then."

The diminutive maid dipped a curtsey and led us up two flights of stone steps to a long corridor with dark wood doors opening off it.

Mine was third on the left and had an ivory plaque with 'Narraghmore' burned into it. Cara opened the door for me and walked off up the landing with Daniel.

My room reflected the house exterior.

There was a carved dark-wood bed with gold-fringed velvet hangings which had seen better days but the white cotton sheets and pillowcases where starched and pristine.

My suitcases were laid neatly at its foot. Just how had Domnall managed to get here before us? I had no idea.

There were a couple of lamps – I was delighted to see there was electricity – but the room was mostly lit by a roaring fire. The flagged floor was covered with a peculiar mixture of rag and Persian rugs.

A door to the right of the bed led to a modern shower-room. This sure was a crazy house.

I showered, changed and plaited my hair before creeping down the stairs to the hall, half- expecting a gentleman in a cloak with big teeth to sally round the corner at any moment.

I paused in the hall, arrested by a strident conversation from a room across, its door ajar. Dan had tiptoed downstairs and we stood together listening.

It was a heated exchange between Cathal and a person with a very loud hoarse voice and an intermittent lisp.

"Not exactly a welcoming committee," Dan whispered.

"No," I agreed. "No flags and tickertape, that's for sure."

"This way if you please. Mr. Brian is expecting you," said a man servant, his face a mask as he pushed open the door.

The person in conversation with Cathal was issuing instructions:

"We don't have enough for two more. They're not to take horses, do you hear nephew. No horses. They're our collateral – remember that word, boy. It impresses bankers, so it does. Sit, girl!" he ordered Neave, "You're going nowhere. I may have need of you later."

"Miss Bridget O'Neill Sir, and Mr. Daniel Cullen." announced the manservant as we entered the room.

It was unclear whether the 'Sir' was aimed at Cathal or the person I took for Brian O'Neill.

The latter eyed us up and down rudely through a monocle.

"This her?" he asked Neave. "And a Cullen, a CULLEN, as I live and breathe."

She blithely ignored the Cullen reference, and went on:

"Uncle, this is Miss Bridget O'Neill, although she prefers to be called Bridie," said Neave, trying her best to keep a straight face.

"Ah Bridget is it?" he said in a pronounced English accent. "She's not a Donegal O'Neill. Antrim, Tyrone then? I do hope not – thet of no-do-wellth. Not an Antrim gel, are you?" he shouted at me at the top of his voice. "If you are – bugger off!"

"Now, now, Uncle," grinned Neave, "The O'Neill's are noted for their hospitality. Don't let the side down."

"To be sure, to be sure," he said reverting to his native accent and spitting into the fire.

"Now little Miss Bridget…."

"Bridie.."

"As you will," he said testily. "Come here, gel. Let me take a good look at you, Eyes not so good, don't yer know." *English?*

" Come on, come on….," he finished impatiently.

As I drew near, Brian put out a hand with long nails, thick and yellow like a horse's hoof, and grabbed my arm, turning me this way and that as if I truly was a prize mare.

"I hope you're not here for money. Poor ath a church mouth, don't ya know."

"Take it easy, Uncle. She's not after your money," chuckled Neave.

Brian sat back in his chair, relieved but suspicious.

"Don't have no money," he said sulkily.

"Lying bastard!" said Neave low enough for him not to overhear.

He suddenly drew a deep breath, and as if he was addressing someone in Australia bellowed:

"Paidrig. PAIDRIG! Get this fucking chair out of here."

He paused then added.

"Don't yer know."

Chapter Nineteen
Pride of Tara

It wasn't until that point I became aware Brian was in a wheelchair.

Paidrig, whose expression appeared to be permanently 'hang-dog' clicked off the chair brake and trudged off, periodically ducking a brandished walking cane.

"I never used to like this," said Cathal gloomily, looking down at the curling smoke of his cigarette and yellow stains on his fingers.

"Oh, cheer up," said the ever-ebullient Neave. "He's not immortal. He'll run that contraption off the North Tower sooner or later."

"He'll have to get it up there first," said Dan with irrefutable logic.

I thought back to the first conversation I'd had with Neave when she said we had no family connection - or at least none she knew of.

I sure hoped she was right with the 'no connection'. If she wasn't, my grandpa could have been one of old Seamus's relatives escaped to America before he was hunted down for his horse-stealing crimes.

I laughed out loud. Just the thought of my mild-mannered father riding like Jessie James into the Valentine farmyard was so ridiculous.

Cathal looked affronted.

"In actual fact you were an oversight. It was Daniel we wanted."

"Oh stop, Cathal. She wasn't laughing at *you*, were you Bridie?"

"I was just trying to imagine my Pa stealing horses. Mam would have knocked him into the middle of next week."

"Was your father Irish-born?" asked Neave

"No, His grandparents went to America during the famine. My grandpa was Irish but Pa was American born. My great grandparents were from County Mayo, I've heard."

"You're very quiet Dan," I said to my cousin, who looked deep in thought. "Is anything wrong?"

Before he could answer, Cathal changed the subject abruptly:

"You'll need to be up bright and early Daniel, to see to the horses with me."

"Not so, we two," said Neave, gleefully. "You'll be pleased to know – or probably not - we're to breakfast with the delightful Brian. I hope you like kippers."

I had no idea at all what kippers were.

"Smoked herring with lots of bones," grimaced Neave. "Uncle Brian loves them."

The following morning I *was* up fairly early but Cathal and Daniel were already long gone.

Over breakfast, Brian was considerably more reserved. Indeed, he seemed to have become someone else entirely.

He arrived on his feet leaning heavily on a cane and surprised me by kissing my cheek.

"Top o' the mornin' to you, Bridie my dear," he said, tweaking my nose as if I was a toddler. "I hope you're partial to kippers. Love them myself."

"I can't say, Mr. O'Neill. I've never had the pleasure of tasting them."

"Then we must remedy that, toute de suite." *French too, fancy that!*

Neave entered and asked about the kippers. Brian beamed.

"Good morning, Uncle. You're looking chirpy this morning. Sleep well?"

"Capital. Come along Katy Cooper. Father's English," he winked broadly at me, as if that explained the poor girl's deficiencies. "Two of the smokies this morning, I think – plenty of pepper. One for Miss Bridie – to start with."

Kate obediently lifted the lid on one of a row of silver serving dishes.

"Mustard, Sir?"

"Naturally…., of course."

The very idea of fish for breakfast made me feel queasy – fish with mustard sounded disgusting but it seemed rude to say no.

"Scrambled eggs, Katy – and toast," said Neave smiling to herself at my discomfort.

"Will you be taking a walk with us this morning, Uncle? I thought to take Bridie down to the south pasture. Perhaps Cathal and Daniel will be there."

"No doubt mooning over that murderous beast of his," said Brian buttering a piece of toast.

He lay a serviette across his lap and promptly dropped a large piece of buttery kipper down his vest.

"Damn and blast, don't you know!" he said, annoyed.

"Here, let me help you," said Neave, spitting on her napkin and rubbing at his clothing.

"Got to finish the books for the accountant," announced Brian, pushing her away. "The government don't like it if the accounts are late. Damn excise bastards. Can't do with them…., can't stomach them at all."

He dropped his knife and fork with a clatter on his half-eaten fish and strode from the room – an elderly dandy with a kipper-stained vest.

"Take this awful stuff away Kate, and fetch Miss Bridie some eggs," Neave instructed the maid, then to me. "The last time he did accounts for anyone was before Seamus died - grandpa may have been lacking in other respects but he had the good sense to see to *our* survival. His brother's been going dotty for years."

"You are both very good to him. It must be difficult – especially for Cathal."

"Yes. It does rather strike at his authority."

Domnall entered.

"Miss Neave, Ma'am. Mr. Cathal asks would you and Miss Bridget O'Neill come round to the stable yard if you please. He has something to show you…, he says."

Neave was detained momentarily by one of the servants, so I was alone when Domnall 'delivered' me to his master.

The enclosure was large and cobbled and currently held just one horse, which a young groom had by a rope halter.

I'd never seen an animal quite like it and clearly Danny had fallen in love. Cathal stood to one side, grey eyes soft with emotion.

I thought of Daniel's description of Dempsey and Aidan's attachment to him.

This clearly was Cathal's Dempsey.

"This is Pride of Tara – but to me his name is Ghost. He's seventeen hands of lethal muscle," he said with pride.

Indeed the dappled horse was magnificent and with mane and tale flowing, pranced whinnying in the hands of a groom who was having difficulty holding him.

Dan moved to help but Cathal pulled him back in alarm.

"You don't understand, boy. He's wild."

Dan slowly and with care removed Cathal's hand from his arm.

He then did something I thought very strange. He turned and hugged Cathal tightly for some seconds before whispering in his ear.

Cathal nodded and, taking the horse's halter from the groom, motioned for him to leave the yard.

The horse neighed and took several dancing steps backwards.

Dan moved towards Ghost slowly and warily at an angle so the horse could see every step of his approach. He gently took the harness from Cathal's hands.

Ghost was still nervously champing and tossing his head. Daniel pulled down on the harness as the horse calmed, scratching his nose and whispering in his ear until he quietened enough to be walked round the yard.

It must have taken nearly thirty minutes start to finish before the horse was calm and acquiescent in my cousin's hands. I'd never seen such skill and empathy in my life, even on Uncle Conn's farm. Neither had Cathal by his expression.

We all stood still for a few seconds whilst Ghost bowed his head and ruffled Danny's hair.

"He doesn't like grooms," said Daniel quietly and led Ghost back to his stall.

Cathal stood at the gate as Dan latched it.

"I never would have believed it if I hadn't seen it for myself. Even I can't make him behave like that."

Daniel smiled shyly at the compliment.

Then Ghost reared on his hind legs, kicking and thrashing at the wooden door until it began to splinter. An awful wet thud sounded on the gravel at the house front and Neave screamed.

¹ fool

Chapter Twenty
Goodbye to the Last of his Generation

It was history of a day in New York repeating itself. The cobbles were a mess of gore with one leg still intact hanging from a boot-scraper by the front door.

Neave was traumatized, screaming over and over. The rest of us seemed to be stuck fast to the cobbles, heads bent to stare round the corner of the tower.

Nobody moved. Everybody stared down at the remains of Uncle Brian, bent and broken, kipper stain still evident on his torn vest. He'd apparently jumped off the tower Dan had assumed he couldn't climb.

Oddly, it was Danny who reacted first – he was nervous of the unusual, a gentle country boy at heart. But his horror was overcome by pity for poor Neave who was the only one of us who had seen the whole thing, start to finish.

Dan took off his jacket and threw it over the broken head of poor Uncle Brian. He caught Neave as she stumbled, and half-carried her through the door.

Cathal was drawn up to his full considerable height, stiff and pallid as a corpse himself. He steadied himself against the wall then turned and strode back to the stables without looking back.

Since I was the only one even remotely '*compos mentis*', it was left to me to clear up the mess which had been Uncle Brian.

I sent Domnall, relieved he wouldn't have to do the job himself, down to the nearest village to fetch the undertaker.

Meanwhile, it had started to rain heavily and I had visions of poor Uncle Brian disappearing down the nearest drain, leaving behind his leg and monocle.

I shuddered and dashed inside, gratefully accepting the large tumbler of brandy someone stuck in my hand. I took a big swallow and went to help Neave, who now the shock was fading and reality setting in, had sunk onto the dining room carpet in a faint.

The poor old man was left outside next to the steps, quite alone, but there was no reason for us all to be soaking wet so we awaited the funeral director under cover.

After a while, I noticed Cathal was still missing. I told Dan to stay with Neave, and skirting the messy yard, went to the stables, which was the last place I'd seen him.

There were one or two horses, chewing disinterestedly on mouthfuls of hay. Ghost was at the far end of the stalls, shifting and whickering nervously.

That's where I found Cathal. He was sitting with his knees drawn up to his chin and took no notice when I drew back the bolt and sat down beside him on the straw.

Ghost stamped his foot but was otherwise unusually quiet.

We sat side by side in silence for a few minutes, then Cathal took my hand and said earnestly:

"What did I do? What did I do, Bridie to make him act like this? I have always done my best to see he was looked after. Surely it can't have been such a heavy load for him to bear. If I was cruel I didn't intend it."

"You made the best of a bad job I reckon. The old man was clearly crazy. Who knows what he was thinking when he jumped. He may have imagined he was going for a swim in the river – you would know better than I.

"On the other hand he just might have got tired of it all. When he was lucid he'd have been daft err..not to have realized how inconvenient he was."

Cathal buried his face in his hands and I realized how callous that sounded.

"Sorry….," I began but I was interrupted.

"Thank you, Bridie. Every word you said was true although I never would have found the courage to admit it. He was a damned nuisance and my life – Neave's even more so – will be simpler for his passing.

"Now the initial shock has worn off, the guilt I feel is hard to bear," he sighed. "But now there are things to be done."

The first event after any death in Ireland is the organizing of a wake. Cathal was a chief in the O'Neill hierarchy - sort of in the middle - not the top but also not at the bottom of the heap either.

I was as much help as I could be since poor Neave had taken to her bed. I noticed Daniel spent every spare moment with her holding her hand and whispering words of comfort.

The wake was something of a dismal affair, partly because of the lack of a body to display, and partly because the only mourners apart from ourselves and the servants, were over seventy and past the usual pranks and jests.

As neither Neave nor Cathal were feeling on top of the world, it was a gloomy experience, but we could turn the mirrors to the wall and shut the curtains as decreed by tradition.

Alcohol was provided and mourners brought their own offerings but there was as much left at the end as the beginning.

Thank God it was over with quickly.

As the coffin contained only a leg and head it was somewhat shorter than usual so the following day it was carried by four pall-bearers to the church, rather than the usual six. The Mass and interment in the family cemetery was a brief, melancholy affair held in a continuing downpour and soon over with.

Everyone went home.

We had a quick toast to Uncle Brian and retired to our rooms where I slept until early morning.

Chapter Twenty-one
The Beginnings of a Plan

Next day I was up and about before Cara could fetch my cup of tea, but I could hear the usual banging and clattering through the kitchen door as a new day began.

I dressed in my warmest clothes and walked round to the stable yard for some quiet time with the horses before another miserable day began.

I'd thought to spend some time alone, but Danny was there before me, grooming Ghost, which formerly wild, was now putty in his hands.

"Couldn't sleep," Dan said. "Too depressed. I'll ask Cathal if I can take Ghost out for some exercise later. He's tetchy from being inside."

"He'll say no," I shrugged. "He's the same with Ghost as Aidan was with Dempsey."

"I know. It was just something to say."

There was an uncomfortable silence while Dan tackled Ghost's mane, already knot-free.

I was sauntering the length of the stables, patting a head here, scratching a nose there, when Cathal entered in an immaculate tweed riding jacket and stock, tugging at the cuffs and looking ashen but businesslike.

"Ah good! You're here," he said to Dan, brusquely. "I'll saddle Ghost – you go get one of the others – Daisy'll do. She could do with a gallop."

Daisy? Wasn't that the name of a cow?

"Margherita - Daisy!" he said impatiently at my look of confusion.

Nope – not ringing any bells.

"Do you ride?" he asked me, expecting a negative answer.

"Of course I do. I lived in Wicklow with the Cullen and Valentine families. I probably ride as well as you do!"

Danny winced and Cathal treated the remark with the contempt it deserved.

"Well, we'll see about that, won't we? Get Heather ready…..Heather of the Lough! *In ainm Dé….* In God's name, get on with it!"

Right, which was Heather of the Lough?

"The bay… the bay… second stall in."

Once we were walking our mounts to the north pasture, delicate feet clopping, bridles jingling, Cathal turned to Dan and said:

"I have a matter of some urgency to discuss with the two of you when we return. I have in mind to right a wrong and need your help. It will require a deal of subterfuge… and secrecy. And you will have to lie through your teeth to your family."

I threw back my head and laughed. He clearly hadn't met my aunt and uncle.

"Not going to happen. Neither of us have told an untruth to Uncle Conn in our lives and Aunt Siobhan will suss out a lie in seconds."

Dan dismounted and opened the five-bar gate into a mown and levelled practice track perhaps a quarter mile long.

Cathal kicked Ghost into a full gallop.

Lord, that horse was gorgeous. Its hooves measured the ground, tail streaming, moving so fast he seemed to blur.

Cathal was a big man but Ghost carried him with ease, his haunches bunched and head down. They moved as one.

I saw Danny, one foot to his stirrup, hand on the saddle horn arrested in mid-mount as he watched horse and rider arrive at the end of the track.

Cathal was too far away to hear but he stood in his stirrups and waved us forward.

I went next, pushing Heather to her limit but our performance came nowhere close to matching Cathal's. I was being taught a lesson in humility, but had no time to consider this, as Danny was thundering down the track towards us.

I heard Cathal, beside me, give a grunt of approval.

"Good man," he said, ignoring me completely.

Once back at the Tower and the horses groomed and fed, we took a little time to ourselves then assembled for dinner.

We were all there – Neave, Cathal, Daniel and me. There was a great glaring gap where Brian's wheelchair used to be. No-one had the heart to move into it.

Once we'd eaten, Cathal dragged his chair to the head of the table and regarded us all one by one, fixing us with his stare.

"You already know the bare bones of Seamus's activities, Time to put in some detail."

Even Neave, lately recovered and still pasty-faced, looked interested.

"Edmond Valentine, Niall's father, was a hard man when it came to his livestock and spent huge sums of money, particularly in finding and buying mares with pedigrees back to the beach riding of the 1800s. The delight of his life was a stallion which had increased his wealth ten-fold - first as a runner then at stud. His name was Dempsey's Marauder."

Both Dan and I sat up straight and looked at each other in surprise. We hadn't realized Niall Valentine was such a wealthy man. We thought of him just as Uncle Conn's good friend.

"Niall's son, Aidan is my closest friend and Bridie's intended – well..., sort of," said a wide-eyed Dan. "He raised a horse only he could control from a colt; Its name was.... Dempsey."

"Then I guess the Marauder will have been his grandsire. That makes what I'm about to suggest even more important," said Cathal. "I surely would love to see that animal for myself," he added wistfully.

"Well, you're out of luck there," I said. "He was shot through the head by one of the villagers in Cordonagh after Aidan accidentally backed Dempsey into his daughter."

"She survived," said Daniel, the suppressed memory surfacing and making him belligerent.

"Yes, she did, for just short of a twelve-month and even then Mr. Valentine had to pay Joe Doyle a handsome sum to stop him calling the Garda."

This had become a conversation within a conversation so Cathal drew our attention back to the matter in hand.

"My grandfather's actions have filled me with grief and shame since I was a small boy. I have listened to family members recount his actions laughing into their whisky as if he was a folk hero. Our father was embarrassed to carry his blood in his veins.

"I have to think of some way to make amends. I must.... I must. I can see no other way but....," he murmured, distraught. "I need to go and see if I can think of something else. I don't know if I can do that...,"

Neave put a hand on her brother's arm and he turned his face to her. It was clear she understood his anguish although Dan and I were completely in the dark.

Chapter Twenty-two
Generations of O'Neills

Infuriatingly, at that moment there was a loud bang on the door and without a by your leave, Domnall strolled in but stopped short when he realized his 'mistake'.

"Beg pardon, Sir. I had no intention to interrupt your private conversation."

To me he looked as if he wished he'd entered a while earlier.

"Yes…yes, what is it?" said Cathal, pulling himself together impatiently.

"The funeral man has called with his account. He's requesting payment."

"Tell him I'll be by in the morning to settle with him."

"Tried that Sir. He says there's a bad outbreak of the hinfluenza in Ballynastail and he needs the cash."

Cathal stood and pushed back his chair with such force it hit the wall behind him.

"I beg your pardon ladies and gentleman. I'll deal with this and be back directly."

Domnall tugged his forelock and loped out of the room, Cathal following close behind.

"Goddam!" I exclaimed reverting to Manhattan-ese in my disappointment. "Just when it was getting interesting!"

Cathal returned a half hour later looking harassed and annoyed.

He resumed his account:

"Seamus may just simply have reckoned on the Donegal O'Neills being clear across the island from the Valentines.

"But I think it more likely the Valentines had something to do with the fearsome scar Seamus carried to his dying day – it ran from here to here," said Cathal, drawing a line from his brow to the corner of his nose."

"You can see for yourself. Seamus's mother had the portraits of all her children painted. They're on the north staircase," said Neave.

"Come," she said, still a little wobbly on her feet. As Cathal took her arm, I saw her glance momentarily at Daniel.

We followed them the length of the tessellated hall to a stairway which seemed to lead towards the ruined north tower.

At the top, it was blocked by a solid door, securely locked.

Along the length of the dark stairway was a series of small, gloomy oil paintings, which seemed not to have seen the light of day in a good while.

"Brian," said Neave, indicating the first canvas. "Sad that such a handsome boy should end up so completely unhinged."

He really was good looking, with soft blue eyes and the appearance of a dreamer about him. Not at all the hardnosed money man he became.

"Cormac," she continued. "Liked the ladies. There are a few children in the village still, with his red hair and high cheekbones."

"Colin - even nastier then Seamus."

It was true there was a cruelty about his down-turned mouth and direct stare.

"The delightful Seamus," said Neave, pulling a face. "Bonny, isn't he?"

The truth was he could have been, but for the gash running across his cheek. It was so deep as to have healed laid open. He had eyes of an indeterminate color, heavy-lidded and piercing and the same curling russet hair as Cathal.

Neave searched through the paintings:

"This is our mystery portrait. Only Brian knew who she was, but he's taken that particular secret to the grave."

The portrait was set a little apart from the others and was better executed. It showed a truly beautiful young girl with high cheekbones, and a full-lipped mouth with a pronounced cupid's bow. Her soft blond hair was swept upwards into a bun on the crown of her head, and she wore delicate pearl drop earrings.

"I've sometimes wondered if she wasn't the cause of a feud between the O'Neills and Valentines. It would give some basis for subsequent events," said Neave, always ready for a bit of romance, even if it wasn't warranted.

Cathal brought several pieces of paper from the sitting room desk and laid them out on the table.

He pulled the first sheet towards him and began to write, occasionally screwing up the paper, throwing it on the floor in frustration and starting anew.

The end result, after a number of false starts read as follows:

O'Neill Family

1. Seamus *born Jun 1ˢᵗ, 1841,*

(i) m.4 Jan 1878 **Caroline (Kitty) Mickley**

      2. Unknown - rumor

(ii) m.12 Oct 1879 **Dorothea Moran**

      2. Liam *born May 31 1880,*

        m. Oct 26ᵗʰ 1899, **Jeannie Graham**

          3. **Cathal born 21 Dec 1900**

          *3.***Neave born 17 Apr 1902**

          3 Still-born twins 1904

      2. Arthur *born 1882 died in Australia*

1. Cormac m. Maria Bailey

      2. Jane (died of cholera aged 9),

      2 Finbar (killed by the English),

1.Colin m. Neave O'Mally

      2.Bessie
      2. James
      2. Dermot

1. Brian (never married)

Cathal scratched his head.

"I haven't bothered with all the brothers' extended families. It's confusing enough as it is.

"Seamus's parents died soon after Brian's birth and Seamus inherited the title of O'Neill chief, which gave him *carte blanche* to do as he liked. There was no-one around to object when he began training the whole family's boys for the horses."

Neave took up the tale:

"Caroline, Seamus's first wife – Kitty he called her – he married for love. There was talk in the family that there was a child but it was only a rumor. Perhaps it died - I don't know."

"Our father," continued Cathal, "was Liam, Seamus's older son. Our mother was Jeannie Graham.

"Neave and I also had twin brothers who were stillborn so unnamed. Our poor mother died with them.

"The Lord alone knows what happened to Colin's kids – he probably beat them to death like he did his wife. He was hung in Mountjoy jail in Dublin. In a family of villains, Colin was the worst. Our mother kept us well away from him so I never knew him or his family."

Cathal was embarrassed by this revelation, it was plain to see. He had flushed and his strong hands gripped the table edge.

"I trust in your discretion," he said to Daniel and me. "I've never in my life spoken of this to a soul. *Impím ort!*"

"I implore you..." translated Neave in a whisper. Cathal took a deep breath. I was standing next to him so could do no other than to wrap my arms around his waist for comfort. He hugged me back.

"*Cailín deas*," he whispered.

Neave clasped her hands together– I could only imagine it was something romantic. "Sweet girl," she mouthed.

I said softly:

"You know, Cathal O'Neil, your life would be a damn sight easier if you spoke to me in a language I could understand."

"[1]*Seans ar bith*," he said into my hair and I could feel his smile.

"We've to try and figure out what we can of the Valentines next," said Cathal, "but for now, if you'll excuse me, I'm going to bed. My head aches."

[1] Not a chance

Chapter Twenty-three
...... And What of the Valentines?

When Dan didn't appear for breakfast the following morning, I went and banged on his door.

At a distracted 'Yeah', I entered and found him sitting on his unmade bed with a few sheets of paper and a pencil, trying to emulate the diagram Cathal had constructed the previous evening.

By the look of the crossings-out and the screwed up paper on the floor, he was doing a lousy job.

"I don't know anything!" he said despondently. "I'm really trying."

"Not wrong there," I teased, taking the current sheet before he could dispose of it.

Across the top was written:

"Valentine ~~Fem~~ Family"

Edmond Valentine m. unknown

> *Only child (I think) Niall m. Eefa not sure*
> *Rosalind, Aidan*

"And you missed bacon and eggs for *this*?" I tossed the paper back onto the rumpled sheets. "Aidan's supposed to be your bosom buddy. What in hell do you talk about?"

119

"Horses mostly," he said – it had been a ridiculous question. "Sometimes girls or whisky…. sometimes breeding."

"Which? Girls or horses?" I said, throwing my hands up in frustration.

"Well, wise-guy," he returned defensively, "anything to add? You're supposed to be Aidan's intended."

He pushed the paper and pencil back into my hands.

But I had no clue either.

"Shit! What time is it?", said Danny, ricocheting from the bed.

"Eight-thirty," I said, peering at the little cloisonné clock on the mantle shelf. "If that's right."

"I was supposed to be seeing to the horses' feed. Cathal will be furious!"

"What do you care? You didn't want to come. If I recall rightly he's a 'murdering bastard' you wouldn't go to Ireland with – yet here you are panicking because you might be late seeing to the 'murdering bastard's' livestock."

The last bit was a waste of breath since he was already halfway down the stairs, pulling on his jacket as he ran.

I picked up his useless attempt at understanding the Valentine family and threw it in the fire.

Neave was in the kitchen speaking to the cook so I did a bit of exploring and ended up in the library.

It had the dusty, disused smell of old parchment. When I pulled out a couple of the books, I found the opening pages were lightly foxed from damp.

I wondered why it had been so neglected. The stone-flagged floors, despite thick rugs, made the room very cold. It was clearly an age since a fire had been lit, as both hearth and chimney had been swept clean and covered by an old-fashioned embroidered screen.

Leatherbound books, some tooled and edged in worn gold, lined the shelves.

My attention was drawn to three volumes in faded cloth bindings. They were on a high shelf and so different from the rest of the expensive covers they piqued my curiosity.

I pulled one down and saw it was volume one of "Pride and Prejudice". The beginning pages were starting to loosen but I was able to see from the frontispiece it had been published in 1813 in London. I dusted off the other two volumes and saw they were indeed a set.

"Ah, there you are," smiled Neave from the doorway. "Come and have some tea in the parlor – it's the warmest spot in this spooky old house. Bring your books if you like."

I showed her what I'd found.

"Well spotted – you must have an eye for these things considering the rubbish there is in here. A first edition Jane Austen - I didn't know we had such a thing. Take them if you want - they're a bit of a mess."

I must have been gaping like a fish because she giggled delightedly.

"Oh, go on…they're only raggedy, smelly old books!"

"I've never seen such old books - I'd like to take a look for myself. If it's okay with you, I'd like to give them to Dan's sister - my cousin - Molly. She'd be over the moon."

Later that evening, as the rain beat against the windowpanes I curled up next to the fire in my room to examine my new treasures.

The first book was perhaps the best used. Some of the page edges were turned over to hold the reader's place, and the first couple were grubby..

The second book was in better condition, its spine secure, and it was cleaner and tidier. On the empty page facing the cover was a dedication in copper-plate, faded but clearly discernible.

To my most beloved Kitty

Yours, ever in true fidelity

Edmond Valentine

I was speechless. What did Seamus's wife have to do with Edmond Valentine? Did Neave know? Had Seamus known, more to the point.

It had been by the biggest fluke I happened to pick up that particular book with its dedication.

Chapter Twenty-four
A Horse of a Different Color

"I've decided to take Ghost to Wicklow," announced Cathal, striding across the black and white tiles of the hall and into the sitting room

"WHAT?" said three voices in unison.

It was a measure of Cathal's agitation that he strode across the expensive Persian carpet - practically the only new bit of furnishing in the entire house - in riding boots thick with detritus from the stables.

Neave was about to protest until Cathal spoke those astonishing words.

He threw his leather gloves on an armchair, and unbuttoned his tweed jacket, all the time looking from face to face as if to dare opposition.

"Why?" I asked, speaking for the whole room.

"When Seamus took Edmond Valentine's herd, he took everything but one brood mare, which was in another pasture as she was about to foal. Dempsey's King, off-spring of Dempsey's Marauder and sire of your friend's horse.

"Ghost's dam was another of Edmond's brood mares. She could trace her direct line back to the first Irish racers. She was found to be in foal by Dempsey's Marauder not long after Seamus got back here - it's a miracle they both survived."

"Oh Lord above!" I exclaimed

"Shit! Sorry Neave," said Daniel. "Ghost's grandsire was also Dempsey's!"

"Yes, so it would seem," said Cathal, "In all decency Ghost belongs to Niall Valentine since both lines of his pedigree rightfully belonged to him."

"But he's *your* horse.!" exclaimed Neave, aghast. "You would never have dreamed of selling him - you wouldn't even run him - and now you'll give him away?"

"How else will I get to Mr. Valentine? I have to interest him in Ghost before he learns we're Seamus's grandchildren or we'll never work this out."

"Why is this so important to you?" I asked perplexed. "You're taking a lot of chances to right a wrong done so long ago - and not by you or Neave."

Cathal stalked from the room, head down. Dan made a move to follow him, understanding perhaps as no-one else in the room did, what Ghost meant to Cathal, but Neave stopped him.

"He needs to be alone to work this through. You have no idea what that pronouncement has cost him. Even more than the usual love of a boy for his first horse, Ghost came to him as a result of our father's Will, but as Cathal sees it, he owns him under false pretenses. In his eyes, he can never truly own him without Niall Valentine's agreement.

Later, Daniel did go looking for Cathal, but he had saddled Ghost and taken him out of the stables.

I spent the afternoon in the rather Spartan gardens which surrounded the Tower, trying to work out what I knew about Seamus's first wife.

Her name was Caroline but it appeared Seamus wasn't the only one to call her Kitty - Edmond Valentine had too.

I kicked a large stone into a hedge in frustration and nearly broke my toe.

I could think of nothing other to do than take what I'd found to Neave and ask her thoughts.

Cathal was out, Dan in the stables and Domnall for the moment had his nose in someone else's business. I collected the books from my room and tracked Neave back to her little parlor next to the kitchen, where - of all things - she was pulling scraps of material through old sacking with a hook. She put it aside as I came in.

"Nice rug," I said, raising my eyebrows. "I have some questions for you."

"Fire away - it looks serious.

"When I was poking around in the library and found the Austen books, this was written inside the second volume."

I handed it to her and saw her eyes open wide in surprise.

"I didn't know they'd even met. Perhaps Cathal might know more. I'd leave it today though. He's not in the best of moods."

Chapter Twenty-five
The Road to Cordonagh

I found Cathal in his office the next morning, looking white and drawn. Dan stood beside him nervously.

"What? WHAT?" said Cathal irascibly as I walked through the door. "What now… what do you want?"

"I beg pardon your Royal Highness," and I curtseyed, glowering. "When would be convenient Sire?"

He threw his pen down on the blotter, folded his hands on the desk and waited pointedly for me to speak. When I paused, Cathal motioned for Dan to leave.

I opened the book and laid it on his desk.

"What the hell!" he exclaimed. "Where did you find that?"

"It was in your library."

"No-one's been in there in years. The books were bought by Seamus's mother, but pretty much abandoned after her death."

"Not completely it would seem."

"If Kitty had need to hide the books, where could have been better than a library nobody used," mused Cathal.

"I've put this off long enough. Find Neave and get your things together. We leave tomorrow for Wicklow. We needs some long overdue answers about the Valentines - and the O'Neills."

Transporting horses right across Ireland was not an easy operation, and had to be done by road in stages, so Cathal's 'we leave tomorrow' made Neave laugh out loud.

"It'll take a week to prepare and ten days to get there!"

It did, and we looked like a platoon of soldiers marching off to war. Besides Ghost, there were mounts for each of us and feed and tack; veterinary equipment organized by Daniel 'just in case'. There were clothes, outdoor and in, for the four of us - no grooms because Ghost was so in fear of them - we'd have to do their work between us.

We'd to stop daily to allow both horses and ourselves to feed and rest, which apart from one night when we came across a small village with a pub, meant camping out. And on top of all that, we'd to skirt that Godforsaken border and keep out of the way of the guards.

By the time we got to Wicklow I never wanted to see a goddam horse again as long as I lived - nor most of Ireland either.

I'd managed to get a letter off to Uncle Conn before we left. He met us on the road south of Dublin city and helped us unload our - by this time - ramshackled, mud-besplattered belongings into a smart new truck with

'Connell Cullen & Sons - Horse Breeders and Dealers'

stenciled neatly on the side in green and cream.

"We've proper roads now," he said by way of explanation as he hugged Dan and me warmly and tentatively shook hands with the O'Neills, who I'd told Uncle Conn were cousins of my father. He huffed and told us to let him know their name once we'd changed it.

A weary Dan with Cathal walked the equally exhausted horses the last miles to Cordonagh.

If the greeting we got from Conn was warm, Siobhan's was red hot. She jumped up and down and laughed and cried.

So did her eldest son, the tears making runnels down his dirty cheeks.

"You can have my bed," said a little voice behind me and I turned to see my beautiful Rosie, her chestnut curls tied up in a blue ribbon and her cheeks glowing from the fresh air.

"Little squirt's going to be the most beautiful of us all," laughed another familiar voice - Rosheen in her boots and overalls, her long Titian hair tied in thick plaits and a bucket of oats in her hands.

Chapter Twenty-six
The O'Neills Meet the Cullens

I was asleep before my head hit Rosie's pillow, and I awoke as on the very first night I'd spent at 'Long Barrow' to Rosie sitting on the bottom of the bed crunching on an apple.

"We thought you was dead. Pasty, ain't you?"

How wonderful such a small remark had been so important to us both.

We howled so loud with laughter Auntie Siobhan ran in holding the bread paddle wondering what on earth was going on.

"Rosie, go cut the bacon for breakfast," she said. "We've guests so cut plenty. Have the hens been seen to? We need eggs. Two dozen if there are that many."

Demoted to hen-duty again, poor Rosie.

"And you needn't think you can loll there like Mata Hari," she said to me. "Get up and set the table. For… "she stopped to count, "eleven."

"Twelve." I corrected.

Aunt Siobhan raised her eyes to the heavens, hands clasped in despair.

"Oh blessed Jesus…" she groaned, running as fast as her girth would allow through the door.

I sorted out some fresh clothes, brushed and plaited my hair, and went to wash and clean my teeth under the tap in the yard.

"Very elegant.." shouted Cathal at the sight of my posterior as I bent to rinse my face. He and Dan had settled the horses then slept the night in the stables.

"At least I don't look like a scarecrow," I yelled back, and mimed pulling stalks from my hair.

Dan drew a strand from his own and put it between his teeth, grinning at me:

"Oh Lord, what will your parents think of me. I must look like a tramp," said the O'Neill chief in dismay.

"They'll think you slept the night on straw in the stables. Then Mam'll fill you so full of bacon and eggs you won't want to move for a month…. After that she'll tell you you stink like a farmyard and order you to take a bath."

So far, I hadn't seen Neave. She was being treated as a guest so no-one - even Rosie - had woken her. When I went to rouse her myself, she looked like hell.

"Breakfast in ten minutes," I told her. "If you're not there, it'll be bread and jam."

"With tea? That'll do fine. There in twenty."

As I shut the door, there was a thump as she fell out of bed.

Of course, breakfast was a free-for-all. Most of them had been up since near daybreak and were starving, and 'please pass me this, please pass me that' was minimal. Cathal learned to pitch in - either that or go hungry.

Neave when she finally emerged looked so bad Auntie found her a chair and filled her plate herself.

When we'd eaten, everyone sat in the yard enjoying a bright new day, while I spent a happy half hour introducing them all and basking in the sunshine, quietly enjoying the company.

Neave broke the silence by asking if after the long tiring journey, anyone would mind her taking a walk alone for an hour or two. That seemed odd coming from the gregarious Neave. Perhaps she had been more tired than I'd imagined.

"Rosie, it'll be alright if Neave takes Fang with her, won't it?" I asked, and at Neave's dubious expression, "Don't concern yourself. Rosie's dog is a small collie more likely to lick you to death!"

Rosie put a collar and lead on her beloved dog and showed Neave the path over a low hill next to the lane.

Meanwhile, breakfast break complete, I went to help Auntie Siobhan clear the table and clean up the kitchen.

"Can't do with you slacking, *daor*. We need to find you something to do now that Rosie's back on hen-duty. For now, why don't you take a day off? You've had a tiring time."

I went to catch up with Cathal and Dan and found them deep in conversation, watching uncle's herd.

[1]"*Dia dhuit*, Bridie Cullen," my cousin greeted me.

"Cullen?" asked Cathal in surprise.

"It's a year or two on from the Troubles now, but when Bridie first came to us my father changed her name to ours, O'Neill being a northern name and herself foreign to these parts."

"Good point," said Cathal, eyeing me speculatively. To my utter horror, I blushed. His eyes sparkled with suppressed laughter. "What shall we be?"

"What about 'Kennedy' - they're mostly in Galway. Its far away from here," suggested Dan.

"Cathal Kennedy it is then. I'll tell Neave and hope she remembers."

Ghost had been put in a pen to one side of the pasture away from the other livestock. Compared to him, my uncle's carefully reared standards looked like cart horses.

"I'll bring everyone up to help stable them later," said Dan to Cathal. "There's little shelter so we can't chance them out all night."

Neave was back for dinner and helped Rosie feed Fang before she sat down.

Rosie had managed to unload the care of the hens onto Neave. She'd really thought she'd got away with it until auntie gave her the byre to muck out as punishment.

Once the initial euphoria of the homecoming had worn off, Dan seemed down in the mouth, so I wasn't surprised when he decided to ride over to 'Redmile' the following day to see Aidan. He invited me to go with him and I looked to auntie for permission. She waved me away with her hand.

"Can I come too?" asked Cathal. "If it's no more than a few miles I could take Ghost for exercise."

"Coming Neave?" I asked.

"No thanks, I was going to ask if I could walk Fang again. You could come too," she said to Rosie. I thought this was just what Neave needed. Rosie's cheerful company would be good for her.

"Oh no you don't Rosanna Cullen! There's enough of you sloping off - I need help in the dairy - it's churning you'll be doing."

"Rosanna?" I laughed. "Bit fancy for a runt like you, isn't it?"

She stalked off to the dairy behind the byre and a clattering of metal objects could clearly be heard across the yard.

"Jesu - I'd better get to work before she breaks the creamers," said auntie at a run.

We saddled up and walked our horses down the lane to 'Redmile' like Hollywood cowboys - all except Cathal, who on Ghost looked more like Mr. Darcy.

[1] Hello

133

Chapter Twenty-seven
'Redmile' and the Reunion

'Redmile', for a stock farm was a very peaceful and orderly place - pretty even, with its hawthorn hedging and flowerbeds.

The house itself was large, rectangular and covered in ivy. I guessed it was probably contemporary with 'Túr Capaill' although it was difficult to tell with all the greenery climbing its walls.

It was set in a small hollow which widened out to the rear of the substantial house to provide pasture and stabling for a herd of exquisite thoroughbreds, mostly bays but with one or two greys with deeper mottling than Ghost.

Niall and Aidan greeted us at the door and ushered us inside.

As the others walked forwards, Aidan dropped back took my hand, and squeezed it in the folds of my skirt. The look he gave me reminded me of that unpleasant meeting at the dance - almost as if he was claiming ownership. His manner altered however when he noticed the little gold cross around my neck, which I had never removed since he fastened it there himself.

"Lorelei," he whispered in my ear, before dropping my hand and joining in conversation with his father.

Niall was a handsome man in his early sixties. Tall, straight and vigorous, he had diamond-sharp blue eyes and abundant white hair cut close to his skull.

As they were introduced, he grasped Cathal's hand firmly and looked him straight in the eye.

"Good day, young man. Will you take brandy? I have an excellent Cognac…. or would you prefer whisky?"

"Brandy would be good, thank you," said Cathal and I noticed he had adopted a faint New York accent - not strong but just enough to easily notice.

Once everyone was seated, Niall in a leather wingchair next to an open window, he continued:

"Was that your own animal you rode over - or your father's perhaps?"

"He's mine," said Cathal with pride. "With advice from my father, I raised him myself. I saw him flinch as he realized he may be losing Ghost to this man.

"And good day to you too, Bridie," said Niall to me. "It's a year or two now since you took up with this boy of mine. You'd an eye for a fine steed yourself if I remember rightly."

Niall finished his Cognac and said:

"Come Kennedy - let's take a look at this thoroughbred of yours. What's his pedigree? He looks Irish, right enough. I take it your family are breeders.?"

The men's voices receded down the hall and they left me behind with 'the ladies'.

I'd seen Mrs. Valentine once before in fraught circumstances at the dance, but never Aidan's sister Rosalind.

Mrs. Valentine was a straight-backed lady, with unruly white hair plaited and wound round her head like a crown, Her eyes, though she smiled at me, had a sadness about them.

It was Rosalind who came as a real surprise. She was perhaps a year or two older than Aidan. I'd always assumed her seclusion was caused by an unfortunate appearance, but she was quite lovely. She reminded me of someone, but for the life of me I couldn't think who.

That she'd lived a sheltered life was made clear by her old-fashioned clothes which had too much lace to be stylish, and her dress was on the long side, though its particular shade of pale lilac perfectly complemented her unusually light amber eyes and dark blonde hair.

She smiled at me kindly and said in a surprisingly mellow voice:

"Come into the sitting room, Miss Cullen - or would you prefer Bridget?"

"No… please no. The only person who ever called me Bridget was my mother, and usually when I'd done something wrong. Please call me Bridie."

Her laugh had a slight tinkle to it which was most attractive.

"Would you care for tea? I believe coffee is the thing for Americans. We probably have some tucked away somewhere but I wouldn't recommend it. We Irish are notoriously bad with coffee."

Thank the Lord someone at long last realized I wasn't English.

I accepted the tea gratefully.

Mrs. Valentine had yet to speak and seemed content to leave the greetings to her daughter. Now she excused herself politely and bustled off to the kitchen to give instructions to her cook.

Once we were seated I offered Neave's apologies - naturally she hadn't offered any - and asked if I might visit again and introduce her.

"I will have to check with my father. I do hope that won't be inconvenient," said Rosalind doubtfully. She had a lovely voice but her way of speaking was formal and as out of place as her dress.

"I understand my brother has asked for your hand. I would so love a sister for company," said Rosalind.

"I wouldn't exactly say that. It's perhaps wishful thinking by some," I laughed. "But then I was called back to New York. He gave me this gold cross as a memento though."

I held it out for her to see. She noticed the engraving on the reverse and said:

"Lorelei?"

"No idea - he gave it to me as a promise - at least that's what I've always believed."

"Odd choice - Lorelei was a maiden in Teutonic folklore who threw herself into the river over a faithless lover," she smiled, "He never was much of a scholar and probably just thought it was an appealing name for a pretty girl."

Mrs. Valentine entered at that point followed by a maid carrying a tea tray.

I could see where her daughter's manner of speech came from, but there the resemblance ended. Aidan had much of his mother about him - tall and straight although his tone of voice was more softly Irish. Rosalind had inherited very little.

It was quite some time before the men returned

Cathal's plan seemed to be working out better than he'd expected. Mr. Valentine had shown him some carefully selected brood mares he was intending for insemination in the Spring, and had taken Cathal to look them over, and offer an opinion.

Dan had noticed him quietly appraising Ghost on a couple of occasions. So had Cathal.

When we took our leave later that afternoon with a promise to return the following week, Mr. Valentine asked if he could ride Ghost the hundred yards or so to the gate.

We watched as he walked him down, then canter back, leaning slightly to examine his gait.

"When are you going to tell him?" I hissed at Cathal.

"When I'm sure he knows me well enough not to run me off his ranch at gunpoint."

"A beautiful example. Do you intend breeding from him?"

"If the right dam can be found, yes."

Niall dismounted and handed the reins to Cathal then looked at him curiously.

"I know most of the Irish breeders but your family is not one I recognize. I know of no Kennedys in Galway who raise thoroughbreds."

"No Sir," said Cathal and I heard him very slightly raise his accent - perhaps only enough for an American to recognize. "My mother's family are from New York and we've spent some time there, but I attended Newbridge College in Kildare for a number of years. It's not far from Wicklow I believe."

"It isn't, but until the roads improved over the past few years it was a tough journey over the Wicklow mountains or by way of Dublin."

'Thank all the Saints,' I thought, my stomach returning to its proper place.

Aidan helped me into the saddle, and his hand trailed the length of my leg to the ankle as he placed my foot in the stirrup.

Cathal caught my eye and I could see he was displeased by the familiarity. I may love Aidan, but his intimate touch didn't sit well with him at all.

Chapter Twenty-eight
Bridie Confronts Her Sexuality

Dan, Cathal, Neave and I sat in the stables after a hard day's work and held a council of war.

"If we are to carry this off, we need to keep our stories straight. I'll tell you what's been said so far - by me anyway," said Cathal. "You and I, Neave, are Kennedys from Galway. Niall doesn't know us as we've spent some years in America. Then I went to Newbridge College, a private school in County Kildare."

"Bit close to home, don't you think?" said Daniel.

"I did worry about that, especially when Niall said he'd thought of sending Aidan to Newbridge. But he said it was difficult to reach other than by way of Dublin, so he hired private tutors instead.

"You need to very slowly adjust your accent sister, to sound more American."

I looked at Dan. Auntie Siobhan would pick up on that instantly.

"I think we may have to include my mother in our plans. She's too shrewd not to notice," he said. "I'm sure if we explain it properly she'll keep her mouth shut."

"Not a thing she's good at with Uncle Conn," I fretted.

"You're good with her - you do it. She likes you," said my helpful cousin

"You're her son," I countered. "Presumably she does a bit more than *like* you - although I do see your point. But it'll have to be done."

By me as it turned out.

This gave rise to another thought:

"I suggest you're all careful when it comes to Rosie. She's a gob on her like a claxon," I said.

"Truer words were never spoke. Mam and Da it is then." agreed Dan.

Cathal looked about to lose his temper, so I leaned over and gave him a smacking kiss on the cheek.

Seeing a muscular man nearly six and a half feet tall blush, is akin to seeing a dog climb a tree - oddly out of place.

Everyone laughed but Cathal, who looked thoroughly discomforted. What was wrong with him? He never used to be such a bore.

And he wasn't the only one. Whatever had been wrong with Neave, seemed to have spread to Danny. He had a face like a wet weekend.

Which left only me, and possibly Aidan, behaving normally - even Rosheen seemed to be out of sorts. I was going to have to find some way to cut through the gloom.

But the next move turned out to be Mr. Valentine's.

Aidan rode over to invite us all to dinner. When I say all, I mean the grown-ups which included Dan and me. Neave and Cathal were to be guests of honor, of course.

Aidan, who'd known my aunt and uncle his whole life, was taken into the kitchen and treated to a thick slice of treacle tart and a glass of milk. Like Dan, he'd never be allowed to grow up at Long Barrow.

I'd yet to manage a few moments alone with Aidan and I could tell by the intensity of his gaze that was about to be corrected at the first available moment. I twiddled his cross between my fingers and smiled at him.

When it was time to leave, Aidan went to collect his horse from the stables and I followed him. He was scratching between its ears and speaking softly to it.

When he noticed me, he grabbed me by the hand and dragged me inside the building and out of sight of the house. We had both been waiting for this moment since my return.

His kiss was passionate but then so was mine. He pulled us together body to body until I fell against him gasping.

Rosheen walked in dragging a bale of hay for the horses' evening feed. Bit early I thought, fighting to control my breathing. Aidan was leaning against the wall with his head resting against the boards, then he pushed away, mounted his horse and disappeared at a trot down the lane.

"Didn't interrupt anything, did I?" asked Rosheen, guilelessly. "We haven't seen much of Aidan since you and Dan have been away. I expect he was pleased to see you."

There was nothing polite I could say to that, so I brushed straw from my jeans and strode back to the kitchen foaming at the mouth, hot and bothered.

Naturally, my appearance wasn't lost on auntie.

I walked out back of the house, sat on the water barrel and lit a cigarette. Cathal and Neave both smoked so I figured I'd give it a try.

"What's she done?" asked Aunt Siobhan from the doorway behind me.

"Who?" I said blowing out a cloud of smoke and coughing.

"Rosheen - you silly girl. Rosheen - who else? She's been making cows eyes at Aidan ever since you left. To his credit, he's ignored her."

Auntie pulled the cigarette out of my hand and ground it out with her heel.

"You are a tease or stupid, Bridie. Do you look like that on purpose because if you don't you've got real problems. Get off there."

I jumped down from the barrel and tugged at the jeans Dan had given me to work in. They were tight but still I'd to cinch them in at the waist with an old belt to make them stay up.

I looked a mess, I realized. Not only the jeans and belt. But I was wearing an old plaid shirt of Ronan's with a button missing. I'd knotted it above my waist to keep it out of the way while I worked.

It didn't help, I supposed, my hair had worked loose from its braid and flopped over the right side of my face.

"Have you ANY idea what you look like! You could earn a living at Monto for what you're wearing right now."

I looked down at my old work clothes and wondered what Monto was.

"What's Monto?"

"It's where ladies of the night collect to display their wares in Dublin."

For a moment I looked at her blankly. Did she mean what I thought she meant? Did she mean I looked like a whore?

"Can I take a bath and change my clothes then?" I asked not altogether sure I'd responded correctly.

"You can for all the good it'll do. You can't 'make a sow's ear out of a silk purse' any more than you can do the opposite." *What?* "I'll have Dan explain - it's beyond me."

Later that evening, as I was rubbing liniment into a bruised hock, Dan came and leaned over the door looking at me thoughtfully. I went back to my work.

After a moment or two he said:

"Mam say's you're a muppet."

"What's one of those?" I asked, not looking up.

"Eejit - idiot!"

Well, that was plain enough.

"Don't you know you look about as innocent as Evie Nesbit?"

Her I knew - a movie actress with a sordid past.

I picked up a hayfork and hit him over the head with the wooden end.

"I do not!" I said mortified. "Why would you say such a cruel thing?"

"What makes you even more alluring is your innocence. You have absolutely no idea at all the effect you have on men. Thank God I'm your cousin!"

"I do not!" I said, outraged.

"Go take a look at yourself. The tight belt shows off your waist and [1]*do chuid pluide* when you bend down the missing button shows your breasts to your navel, your hair looks as if you just tumbled out of bed after some violent exercise….. and you look as if you should be sucking a lollypop.

"You're driving Aidan insane and Cathal falls over his feet whenever you walk round the corner - which I bet is a first for him. Even Ronan and Craig have noticed. Don't be surprised if you've not many female friends."

"He does not! They have not!"

I bolted up the ladder to the hayloft and hid my face in some old sacking until it itched.

"It's not true - you bastard, Daniel Cullen. It's not true!"

"Sit and think about it, then we'll talk some more - see you later."

He picked up the pitchfork I'd attacked him with and hung it back on its rack.

[1] your thighs

Chapter Twenty-nine
A Dearly Beloved Sister and Friend

It was good to see Dan back on form for once, even though it was at my expense.

I wondered what was eating at him. Because his lack of spirits seemed to coincide with Neave's, I assumed they were connected, but couldn't think why. She was years older than him, so the obvious solution wasn't likely.

After my conversation with Dan in the stables, dinner at 'Redmile' would be a good opportunity to observe both Cathal and Aidan.

Neave had cried off again. She was naturally light-hearted, bubbly even. Now she was overpoweringly morose. Surely there was more to this than her grief for her uncle.

Dinner at the Valentine's was quite formal, so I wore a pale turquoise cocktail dress Neave had bought me on the ship coming over. She roused herself enough to style my hair and pin a matching silk rose behind my ear.

"How lovely you look!" she said, her voice cracking on the final word.

She hurried out, leaving me to do my own makeup. As the end result was likely to be a disaster, I applied a little lipstick and left it at that.

With the exception of Dan, we drove to 'Redmile' in Uncle Conn's beautiful car which appeared to be locked away only to emerge on special occasions.

As the car was full to overflowing, Daniel decided to ride over. He arrived a little later than the rest of us, pants splashed with mud and his smart tuxedo creased from the saddle.

Dan's eyes were popping when he saw Rosalind. Although he'd known her all his life, he hadn't seen her since his early teens and was clearly impressed by the alteration in her appearance.

Rosalind was a vision of loveliness in a crepe de chine gown with a single strand of lustrous pink pearls at her throat. Her hair had been swept up into a honey-colored confection atop her head. Not à la mode but a style entirely her own.

Cathal was immaculately dressed and deep in conversation with Niall, as he offered him a cigarette from a gold monogrammed case and lit it with a matching lighter.

When we were to be seated, I was mesmerized. I had never in my life seen anything so beautiful. It was as if the room was full of stars.

The highly polished table was set with silverware and cut crystal glasses, which captured the light of a dozen or more slender white candles set in small candelabra along the table's length. At intervals, were delicate arrangements of roses and baby's breath.

The only other light in the room was on a sideboard, holding silver chargers which carried a pastry, cut to display beef inside, roast chicken, and fish with a lemon sauce. Additionally there were vegetables I'd never seen before but roast potatoes and carrots, which I had. It would've fed the whole of Dungannon Road.

"Close your mouth," whispered a voice in my ear. "Your tonsils are showing." I looked up to see....

Cathal... it was Cathal? My Lord that was a side of him I'd never seen before. He grinned and held my chair for me to sit.

After he'd moved away to his own seat, I saw Aidan clench his teeth in irritation.

Uncle Conn and Eefa Valentine sat at the table's top and Auntie Siobhan sat with Niall Valentine at its foot. Between, were interspersed the younger folk in an order to encourage conversation and hopefully a little subsequent romance.

So Rosalind sat with Cathal and Aidan was next to me. Of course, Neave had completely screwed up the seating arrangements by her absence or she might have been stuck with Danny.

I took my lead from the other diners and ate my pâté with the knife and fork furthest from my plate.

"Rosalind says she'd like to go riding tomorrow - would you like to join us?" Cathal said to me across the table.

Aidan glared:

"That won't be possible. I've already arranged to take her to the old monastery ruins at Glendalough."

"Rather a long day's ride for a lady, wouldn't you say?" countered Cathal in his best urbane manner.

I'd had enough of this fencing.

"I'm going walking with Neave so there's no problem. Like to come Rosalind?"

"If Papa agrees, I would."

Just as I was about to attack my boeuf en croute and roast potatoes there was a loud bang and Rosheen burst through the door, eyes wide in panic and hair streaming. Everyone stood in alarm.

"Neave's missing. We can't find her."

Rosheen was as tough as nails - it must be serious if she was sobbing like this.

Neave had taken Fang out - up the lanes to the river, she said. It was quite a hike but she'd taken food with her so when she didn't come back for tea, they didn't bother much until it started to get dark.

"Sean went out up the lane with a flash-light to search for her and found Fang, soaked and shivering in the hedge near the road."

Daniel leapt to his feet and shouted:

"What's wrong with you, you stupid [1]*flute*. If it's getting dark you do more than send Sean out with a flashlight!"

Cathal had moved to question Rosheen further.

Rosalind, still seated at the table, tugged at her hair in a nervous gesture, reattaching a loose strand to its clip.

[1]flute - numbskull

We'd to find Neave. This couldn't be achieved in the pitch black on horseback with torches.

Niall had dogs - he rode to hounds - but they'd never been used to hunt down a person in the dead of night.

It was ten o'clock before they finally gave up and admitted defeat. The decision to pack up and leave things until first light was not a difficult one.

Chapter Thirty
Resurrection

It would have been more efficient for us all to search from 'Long Barrow' but there were too many of us to accommodate, so the Valentines arranged to ride over at daybreak - that's if Neave hadn't reappeared by then.

There was always the possibility she'd wandered too far from home and got lost in the dark, but then what of Fang? Surely he'd still have been with her instead of shivering on a grassy verge close to his home.

Cathal was panic-stricken. He took to striding across the yard and walking up and down the lane through the night, getting more and more agitated until Danny, equally worried, saddled up two of the stronger horses and, as the sun crowned the summit of the mountains, they set off alone across pastures bright with new grass.

They'd only crossed a couple of the large fields out towards the river, when we caught up with them, our horses huffing, their breath vapor in the sharp Spring air.

Mr. Valentine and Uncle Conn took charge and split us into three groups. The river was our primary target as that's where Neave said she was heading for her picnic.

The first group, led by Aunt Siobhan and Dan, with Rosheen and Sean, was to comb the slopes above the river, seeking out all the hollows and hidden places along the peaty ridge.

Mr. Valentine led the second, with Aidan and me. We were to search upstream from a rocky crossing, along a deep and still portion of the river, dark with overhanging branches, their roots binding the banks on either side.

Uncle Conn took Cathal.

Rosie had saddled Gealach and stuck to her father like glue, refusing to stay with the other youngsters at 'Long Barrow'.

They took the down-stream path.

There, the riverbed was rocky and the water, crushed into a narrow defile, rushed and swirled between crevices of granite sparkling with quartzite. But it was narrow enough for Cathal to jump to the far bank and they began a slow search down both sides of the torrent. Rosie, much to her anguish was left in charge of the horses.

After an hour or so, Uncle Conn found one of his wife's flour sacks, which Neave used for carrying her picnic, caught in a rocky pool.

There was a shout and Mr. Valentine, who with Aidan had been diving beneath the river's surface, pulled himself from the water and ran to see what had happened, leaving Aidan and me to continue our search. By this time Aidan, numb to the bone from the cold water had dragged himself onto the bank and sat in the sunshine to warm.

I sat beside him to await Niall's return and he put his arm round me. I pushed him away - he was wetting my shirt - but he tightened his grip.

"Will you be mine Bridie?" he murmured in my ear.

"Not exactly the right time and place to press your suit wouldn't you say?" I snapped, thoroughly annoyed. "It might be we're looking for the dead body of my friend."

"Then she won't be in a position to object, will she?" he grinned at me.

I couldn't believe what I was hearing. Here was this good-looking, athletic young man offering for me when he'd just been diving the river searching for a corpse. He lurched to catch me again but my skirt slipped from his fingers as I knocked his hand away.

"I'll come back with your father when I've found out what's going on. Stay here or its likely there'll be another body they'll be searching for."

Cathal had managed to retrieve the cotton bag from the water. It was empty.

"Are you sure this is what she was carrying?" Mr. Valentine asked a sulky Rosie.

"We've no time for your shenanigans, Rosanna Cullen. Answer Mr. Valentine," commanded her father.

"Yes, sir. I watched her make some sandwiches from the ham in the larder box. She put them in that bag. See, the tie's broken and knotted back together so I know that's the one,"

As if to qualify her bad mood, she added: "She nearly killed Fang. I lent him to her so she wouldn't be lonely on her walks, and she didn't look after him."

Mr. Valentine ignored her wailing and her father slapped her bottom.

"Is the bag all there is? Nothing else?" asked Mr. Valentine.

Their conversation was interrupted by the breathless arrival of Rosheen, who took some moments to compose herself before she could continue.

"We found her…. we found her. She was…. "

Cathal grabbed her arm and shook her.

"Is she alright. Tell me….,"

Tears of relief trickled down his cheeks as Rosheen nodded.

"But she's….,"

I reacted first, grabbed Cathal's hand and yelled at Rosheen to lead the way. Everyone else followed, except Rosie who was left with the horses again.

"I'll get you - I'll get every one of you!" she bawled at her father's receding back, then quailed as he turned to glare at her.

Sean had found Neave in a small hollow on the hillside, curled up against the night cold and deeply unconscious.

Daniel had wrapped her in his jacket and was holding her to his chest for warmth, while Sean rubbed her feet to get the blood flowing.

Cathal took Neave gently from Dan's arms and rubbed her cheek against his own in the tenderest gesture which belied what came out of his mouth.

"What possessed you? You scared the crap out of these good people. We've been looking for you since last bloody night. But more to the point you scared *me* to death!"

"Language, Cathal O'N......err, Kennedy!" scowled my aunt who had just arrived, puffing and panting. "It'll be punishment enough when Rosie gets to you for abandoning her dog. [1]*Fillean an feall ar an bfheallaire"*.

So close...so unbelievably close!

Amazingly, this last seemed to bring Neave round. She started to shudder, then suddenly gave her typical giggle.

[2]*"il grá duit deartháir,"* she whispered in Cathal's ear.

We made our way down the hillside like a parade of clergy carrying a relic, with Cathal leading the way. At the bottom, Rosie slapped Neave hard across her legs, burst into tears and said,

"I thought you were dead, you daft cow. And what about my fucking dog?"

My aunt fetched her a clout to put her on the ground.

"Mind your mouth, Rosanna Cullen - or I'll mind it for you!" promised her mother.

[1] Evil returns to the evil-doer
[2] I love you brother

Chapter Thirty-one
So What Happened With Neave?

When we got to Long Barrow, Auntie told Ronan and Craig to go sleep in the stable with Dan and Cathal, changed the bedding with a screwed up face, and had Neave's brother lay her on their bed.

"Then we'll get to the bottom of this, young man - you just see if I don't."

I don't know if he noticed the 'we' turn into 'I' but I did. There *would* be some answers come hell or high water, but first Neave must rest.

Auntie bustled off to see everyone fed.

"Believe me, Neave will need all her strength to stand up to the onslaught to come," I warned Cathal.

"Your aunt is a wonderful human being…..," he began,

"… and not above calling in Father Lynch to read the riot act if it suits her purpose - even though she detests the man. Every one of her kids works to keep on the right side of her, as well they might. You've an experience in store. You saw what happened to Rosie when she stepped out of line. Neave needs to sleep as long as she can."

The entire Cullen household was assembled for the customary family powwow, hands and faces scrubbed, and lined up until Auntie told them to sit.

Neave was then marched from her bed, accompanied by Cathal and seated at the foot of the scrubbed kitchen table like a felon in a police cell. Auntie Siobhan and Uncle Conn were at the head and the kids then arranged themselves on benches along the sides.

It did occur to me Daniel, Rosheen and I were getting too old for this jiggery-pokery, but on reflection I could picture this from Auntie Siobhan until Rosie was fifty or my aunt died, whichever came first.

Siobhan sat and rested elbows and bosoms on the tabletop.

"Well....?" she demanded, looking Neave in the eye.

I saw Neave flinch then straighten her back. I prayed to God she had the sense to keep her mouth shut or she might find herself out on the hills involuntarily - and Cathal with her. He was clenching and unclenching his fists as if for a fight.

I saw Uncle Conn swing back on his chair and smile to himself. He'd have put money on Siobhan against Jack Dempsey. The kids all looked as if they were expecting Armageddon to explode around the 'Long Barrow' kitchen table, but not so Dan.

"I... I....," dithered Neave, looking petrified.

"Well? You what?" demanded auntie.

Cathal probably thought the situation was about as bad as it could get, but everyone else around that table could have put him straight. Dan leapt to his feet in Neave's defense.

"Sit...DOWN" glared his mother banging the flat of her hand loudly on the tabletop. Everyone including Conn jumped.

Siobhan leaned back against her chair.

"I'm waiting."

"NO, Mam! You will listen to me this time. I am *not* to be treated as a child! I will *not* be bullied and I will *not* allow you to scare Neave," Danny said, glowering at his mother over the table. "You, Neave and I will speak. Everyone else will leave."

He should have been awarded the Medal of Honor for outstanding bravery in the face of the enemy.

I couldn't for the moment interpret the expression on Neave's face and was more than a little peeved to be excluded. Cathal felt the same - obviously. Rosie looked mutinous as she always did when she felt excluded.

I had a sudden flash-back to events at Uncle Brian's suicide and began to put two and two together, surprised Cathal hadn't done the same.

As I passed, I squeezed Dan's shoulder and took Neave's face in my hands and kissed her cheek.

"It'll be fine," I mouthed and followed the others outside where Uncle Conn had wasted no time in putting them to work.

"Idle hands are the devils work," said uncle, mixing his metaphors.

Ten excruciating minutes passed, became twenty then thirty.

When I was on the point of sloping off to peek through the kitchen window, auntie flung back the door and yelled:

"You can come back now.... NOW mind you - whoever's out there by the time I count to twenty, stays out there. ONE..TWO,,,,"

I don't think I ever saw so many people run so fast in all my life. They nearly knocked auntie over in their haste. Rosheen was last in, slammed the door, then almost fell, jumping into her seat.

There was a protracted pause. The whole world held its breath, waiting for my aunt's next pronouncement.

Neave's eyes were fixed on her brother's, pleading.

"Congratulate your big brother and his new intended. Subject to Cathal's agreement, naturally," announced Auntie Siobhan.

Every mouth at that table dropped open in amazement with the exception of mine, and Rosie's whose was too full of words to do any such thing.

"I'm going to be an auntie!" she said with eyes like saucers, as usual, putting the cart before the horse.

Daniel was crimson with embarrassment, as his brothers and sisters hooted with laughter.

Cathal had yet to speak a word.

"Given the difference in your ages, is that wise, Neave? Do you need time to consider?" he asked, his serious manner cutting through the hilarity.

"I do not, brother. We just couldn't tell you - we were so afraid of your reaction," whispered Neave.

Cathal took her hand and kissed her fingertips.

"You didn't need to do what you did."

"Mary Joseph and Jesus," scoffed Rosie. "You're a rare set of scaredy-cats. Get the whisky out Pa."

That child was incorrigible but none of us would have swapped her for the world.

"C'mon, daughter," smiled my Auntie at Neave, "Time to get your feet under the table. Put the kettle on and we'll have a nice cup of tea. Rosheen, there's milk in the larder bucket for Rosie."

I swear she bated that child deliberately.

Chapter Thirty-two
Dan Opens his Mouth and Puts His Foot in It.

Unsurprisingly, Danny and his beloved spent the evening gazing at the moon and each other, whilst auntie threatened to tie Rosie to a chair and Rosheen watched them from the dairy window when she should have been filling the churns.

The next morning, Neave asked to visit the Valentines to apologize and was grateful when we offered some moral support by coming with her.

Auntie gave her some scissors and told her to cut roses from the kitchen garden to give to Eefa Valentine as a peace offering. Auntie Siobhan went indoors to call her friend on the new phone and said we'd be over later.

"You needn't be afraid," I said. "If there was a villain in this story its Seamus O'Neill, not Edmond Valentine. Of course, the name could weigh against you…but it's so many years ago now.

"Mrs. Valentine is quiet and polite and you'll love Rosalind. She's fast becoming my friend. She's locked away in that beautiful house by her father. I guess he has his reasons but I can't imagine what they might be.

Neave was very particular about her appearance when she went to meet the Valentines. Always chic, she had me comb and set her blonde waves and managed to apply her lipstick to perfection. She looked more of a country girl by the time we arrived at 'Redmile', having ridden six miles in a stiff breeze.

Only the 'grown-ups' went, as we'd to break the news of the engagement. So it was my aunt and uncle, Dan, Rosheen - now at nineteen considered an adult, Cathal, Neave and myself.

Rosalind's sweetest smile was reserved for Cathal who looked outstandingly handsome in his riding jacket and with his auburn hair swept back from his brow by the wind.

I wondered in passing why, if Dan was right, Cathal never smiled at me as he did at Rosalind at that moment. Often he was curt, as he had been at 'Túr Capaill' just before I showed him the book dedication or found something urgent to do when he saw me walking towards him.

"I brought these for you, ma'am, by way of apology," Neave said to Mrs. Valentine, and held out the flowers, shame-faced. "I have behaved so badly and I do beg your pardon."

Eefa Valentine's face, at first stiff with disapproval, soften into a smile as she took the roses from Neave's hands.

"Come on in, dear. Rosalind and I were just sitting in the sunroom - come through.

She led us to a narrow room, the front of which was entirely made up of windows, and which ran the full width of the house. There were two glass-topped tables, each with wicker chairs and a porcelain vase of pretty wildflowers - buttercups, daisies and cornflowers.

Neave and Rosalind took to each other on sight, as I knew they would. I smiled to myself when I saw Neave take in Rosalind's unfashionable appearance, and the cogs begin to turn; a shopping trip was on the cards. She still hadn't taken on board that Rosalind was virtually house-bound so it would likely be just her and me in Dublin.

I was less than impressed by the way Aidan looked Neave up and down, but then she was a very pretty lady and most men did.

We sat back against soft cushions while Eefa and Rosalind poured tea and served us delicate sandwiches and scones with their own hands.

I saw Auntie sit forward in her chair and kick Uncle Conn none too subtly on the shins.

He near choked on his sandwich but said:

"Yes indeed, Siobhan.

"Daniel has an announcement to make. It may come as a shock."

Auntie kicked him again and pulled a face at his lack of tact.

Danny stood, turned turkey-red and ran his finger round the shirt collar which seemed to be choking him. He reached for Neave's hand and I saw him visibly shaking.

"Mr. Valentine, Ma'am….. Miss Neave O'Neill….

'Oh, shit, the cat sure had scratched its way out of that particular bag!'

There was a prolonged pause and deathly silence, during which time Dan went from puce to pale in seconds.

"Sit, ¹*amadán*!" said his furious mother.

"Am I to take it you're all in on this…this subterfuge?" said

¹ fool

Niall, puffing out his chest in incredulity. "Even you Colin Cullen? If so you can leave my house... leave now and don't ever enter it again! Go! I'll entertain no O'Neills here."

Cathal spoke in a very quiet but authoritative voice which cut through the chaos:

"My family seems to be making a habit of apologizing to you today, Mr. Valentine. I hope I may further impose on your patience and that you will allow me to exonerate Mr. Cullen and his family. The fault is entirely mine.

"I am Cathal O'Neill, Seamus O'Neill's grandson...."

That was as far as he got before Niall called servants and had us all unceremoniously ejected and the door slammed in Uncle Conn's face as he tried to protest.

Neave turned her face to her pony's stirrup and sobbed. Her worst nightmare had come true.

Chapter Thirty-three
I Do My Best to Stick the Pieces Back Together

The following morning my much-loved cousin and companion Danny looked so weary I could have cried for him, but for his problems this time I could offer no comfort.

Neave walked round pale as a ghost with a permanently wobbly chin until Rosie advised her to 'don't be a chump - pull yourself together'. Much to Rosie's confusion, Neave ran off sobbing.

"Well, when I get intended, I won't be such an eejit. I won't care what anyone thinks."

"Go tell that to your mother," I said wryly.

I never thought to see Aunt Siobhan so distraught. She was so upset, she locked herself in the kitchen and made three batches of strawberry jam so she wouldn't have to speak to anyone.

Uncle Conn, good man that he was, walked the horses to pasture with his eldest son, and with Cathal leading Ghost.

Neave for reasons best known to herself, chose to stay with me. I wasn't as bad as Rosie but I wasn't exactly a sympathetic person. I could hold my tongue though and perhaps that's what she needed most of all - quiet company.

There was a stream, it's banks lined with water-cress and kingcups, which ran across the cow fields behind 'Long Barrow'.

It meant hopping the occasional cow pat and ignoring the ruminating beasts, but that aside it was a very pretty and soothing place to stroll. We jumped over an unstable plank someone had put across the water.

"Bridie, can you please help us, Danny and me? I don't know who else to ask for help or what you could do anyway," said a despondent Neave. "But please would you try? Would you speak to Mr. Valentine - maybe persuade him to speak to Cathal?"

"It'd be risky," I said thoughtfully. "Don't forget I'm an O'Neill myself. Not even Aidan knows that - everyone here knows me as Bridie Cullen. But if I'm discovered, your situation would be so much worse."

"Please.... please try," she begged. "But don't tell Mr. Valentine about Ghost - Cathal wants to do that himself."

Now that my ace - Cathal's offer of Ghost - had been taken away, I couldn't imagine how I was going to approach this.

I decided to take Rosheen with me in the hope her chatter may help control my nerves on the journey.

When I went to look for her, now the stables were empty, Rosheen had been given the task of scouring some of the stalls which she hated. She was dripping wet from the hose and the head had just come off the brush she was using to sweep down the walls.

Adopting a cheery smile I sauntered over and stood watching her as she worked, which didn't go down too well.

"Don't just stand there - grab a brush and give me a hand. I've no time for gabbing," she grumbled.

I helped her until I was as wet as she was, by which time she must have thought honor was satisfied and gave me a grudging smile.

"I take it you didn't come here to muck out stalls. What do you want?"

I tucked a stray strand of hair behind my ear and said:

"I honestly wouldn't blame you if you said no - I'd rather have said the same - but Neave has asked me to go and plead the O'Neill cause at 'Redmile'. I'd sooner enter the gates of hell."

"But you're a bloody O'Neill! How does that work?" she hooted, leaning back against the slats of the wall.

"Even Aidan doesn't know that. No-one here knows I'm an O'Neill so that shouldn't be a problem. Anyway, I'm no relation."

"I don't think Niall Valentine will give a damn. One O'Neill is as bad as another as far as he's concerned. His whole life has been blighted by what Seamus did."

"Well, I've told Neave I'll go. I would have liked you to come with me but if you don't feel up to it I'll have to go alone."

Rosheen leaned her brush against the wall.

"It'll give me an excuse not to finish this," she scowled, kicking one of the rubber mats she'd pulled from a stall.

"Help me clear up. Henry's out back - he's got nothing to do. We can double up."

Henry was the farm workhorse - big and daft, but docile. Rosie had named him after a candy bar when she was little.

"Well, that'll make Niall laugh if nothing else does - us riding up to a thoroughbred farm on a cart horse," I said.

"He's got some himself. Though I have to admit they're more impressive than Henry - brushed to a shine and with legs immaculately feathered."

As we dismounted before the Valentine's home, Mrs. Valentine shot out of the door in a panic.

"You can't be here when Niall comes home. He's due any minute. Please go. Please…please."

Rosalind was standing in the doorway, hands clasped tightly together. She and I had formed a real bond and it looked about to unravel in the worst possible way.

"I'm afraid that won't be possible Mrs. Valentine. There are things which need to be said and better by me than the O'Neills."

I crossed my fingers behind my back at my lack of candor.

Niall Valentine, in highly polished riding boots, and twill jodhpurs, leaped from his fine gelding and confronted me, Aidan in his wake. He didn't even acknowledge Rosheen.

"I told you Cullens were not welcome here, since you gave quarter to O'Neills. Get back on that excuse for a horse and ride back the way you came."

"No sir," I said, squaring my shoulders, and with some difficulty looking him in the eye. "I will not until I've had my say."

I thought he would strike me. Rosheen was gripping the back of my shirt, her usual self-confidence evaporating fast.

"I will not, sir," I reiterated.

Aidan had moved to stand next to his sister on the doorstep, fascinated by the exchange.

Niall must have been impressed by my audacity.

"You…. go with Aidan," he barked at Rosheen, "and you…," he poked his index finger hard into my chest, "and *you* hitch that beast to the post yonder then follow me."

He walked into his office, threw his crop on the desk and glared at me.

"I have to speak for my friend Neave, and for that I make no apology. Although tragic, your family history is none of my concern."

Oh Lord, all the demons in hell were about to rain down, but I could think of no other way to deflect Niall's fury from Neave and Cathal.

"I have to tell you sir, that we are guilty of deceiving you in more ways than you suppose."

He sat on the desk and picked up his crop, not looking at me and not speaking.

"My name is Bridie O'Neill. Conn Cullen is my mother's brother."

It suddenly hit me he must have known my mother as a girl before her family emigrated.

"Rose Cullen married an O'Neill?" he said, shocked.

"She did. His name was Robert - Bob - O'Neill. His family were originally from County Mayo and went to America in the Famine. So generations ago. I'm not related to Cathal and Neave. In fact, I'd never met them until a few months ago."

I told him of my destitute childhood and my first visit to Cordonagh, how Daniel and I had come to know the Donegal O'Neills and how Dan had fallen head over heels in love with Seamus's granddaughter.

I also explained that Neave's distress on the mountain came about because she was so afraid of what he, Niall Valentine, would think and do. She had cared so much for Dan she couldn't bear to come between him and his friends and family.

"Neither Cathal nor Neave O'Neill have their grandfather's cruelty," I ended lamely. "My family have accepted the situation although it doesn't sit well with them, and after a stern warning to his sister - Neave is older than Daniel - Cathal came round too."

Mr. Valentine sat grim-faced throughout.

Chapter Thirty-four
The Sticking Continues

"How did your mother come to be destitute?" asked Niall Valentine, for the moment curiosity overcoming rage. "Her father wasn't wealthy but nor was he poor by any stretch of the imagination."

"I really don't know - I was only a child."

He shook himself out of his revery.

"We stray from the subject Miss Bridget O'Neill. You've dealt with the little Miss but what of that bastard Seamus's grandson?"

"Cathal wants to see you himself if you'll agree. I'm just here as an emissary. But I *can* tell you listening to Cathal would be to your advantage."

He humphed and stood from his desk.

"We'll see. The O'Neills owe the Valentines more than they can rightly repay. Mr. Kennedy - or is it O'Neill - has spun another web of lies - for good or ill - which need to be untangled. You will give me time to consider what can be done - if anything - to mend matters. I'll telephone your uncle in a day or two."

There was an uncomfortable pause.

"I'd be greatly indebted to you Mr. Valentine if you'd continue to call me Bridie Cullen. No-one here knows me as anything else, not even Aidan. My uncle changed my name from O'Neill when I first arrived. The troubles were still uppermost in people's minds, and he thought I might be mistaken for the northern family and their English connections. I've been known as Bridie Cullen as long as I've been here."

"That I can do," he said.

Once our business with the Valentines was complete, Rosheen and I unhitched Henry ready for the journey home.

Mr. Valentine was nowhere to be seen and Eefa and Rosalind had gone back indoors.

Aidan remained behind and chatted as we readied ourselves for the journey back to 'Long Barrow'.

Given the situation, he seemed to be in a cheerful frame of mind and stood with his arm around my shoulders, all the while exchanging local news with Rosheen. He gave me the occasional affectionate hug and kissed my cheek as we left.

It was wonderful we were getting back on an even keel again. I'd missed his good humor and strong arms. The awkward moment at the river I shrugged off as an aberration to be forgotten. I'd probably misunderstood.

Aidan helped Rosheen into the saddle, fitting her foot in the stirrup as he had for me. She bent and gave him a quick affectionate kiss, as she took up the reins. Then he lifted me up behind, kissed me quickly and squeezed Rosheen's arm as we trotted on.

I turned and waved as we rode down the drive and thought how wonderful it was to have known someone so long they had become like a brother.

There was one hell of a shouting match going on by the time we got back.

"Where the hell is she? Those stalls were supposed to be scrubbed out and dried ready for the horses. She's fucked off and left without a word to anyone… I'll take my belt to her when she comes back here, so I will!"

Neave did her best to explain but her little voice was no match for my uncle.

"Oh shit! He doesn't lose his temper often, but when he does it doesn't do to interrupt," whispered Rosheen from the bush we were hiding behind. Fortunately, the jingle of Henry's bridle was hidden by the shouting.

We crept twenty yards up the lane, Rosheen removed Henry's bit and we tiptoed round the other side of the house from the stable, put Henry in his paddock and went to enter the house from the back door.

Unfortunately for Rosheen, Aunt Siobhan was standing grim-faced with the bread paddle in her hand. She looked down at it in disgust.

"You're too big to put over my knee madam or believe me I'd be using this on your arse. I don't know where the two of you have been, but it's not important anyway.

"I'm near deaf, Rosie has a sore behind, Craig is hiding behind the pig pen and the Saints alone know where Sean and Ronan are - over yonder hill, if they've the sense they were born with. Now get out there and take your medicine."

She marched us to the corner of the house and gave us an almighty push until we stood not ten yards from Conn Cullen, arms akimbo and spitting fire.

"Keep your gob shut," advised my cousin out of the corner of her mouth as we neared our fate.

"Sorry Da," she said, doing a reasonable impression of contrition. "I'll go fix it now. Sorry."

He fetched her a clout round the ear which sent her reeling..

I'd my Mam's voice, and her temper too:.

"Stop……stop and hold your tongue until you know what you're shouting about."

Every person in that yard, including Uncle Conn and Auntie Siobhan was struck dumb with shock.

"Now I have your attention….," I took at deep breath.

"Rosheen and I went to 'Redmile' to try and smooth things over with Mr. Valentine. We didn't tell you because we knew you'd stop us."

Cathal took a couple of steps towards us in trepidation.

"No we didn't," I said to him. He sighed with relief.

"Neave begged me to go to try and put Mr. Valentine's mind at rest as to our intentions, and to beg his pardon for the trouble she'd caused."

She bowed her head, dejected. In that moment, I so longed to see the friend I'd come to love, and not this worn, pathetic creature. Dan held her to him and she buried her face in the crook of his neck.

"I commend your intentions and condemn your stupidity, foolish girls.," said my aunt to Rosheen and me, "I just hope I don't have to do any smoothing over of my own with the Valentines."

Uncle was half-way to the stables and saddling a horse before she'd finished speaking, Cathal hot on his heels.

"I asked Mr. Valentine to see Cathal," I yelled after him.

They both stopped in their tracks and turned to look at me in horror. I took advantage of the momentary silence and said:

"He promised to telephone within a day or two to give his decision, once he's had time to think it over."

"How in God's name did you manage that?" asked my uncle in amazement, all anger forgotten. "I thought he'd be running us off his property with a shotgun when last we met. He has one hell of a temper."

"I played the sweet innocent," I said, "and before you say more, Rosheen stayed in the garden with Aidan."

"Good job Niall didn't hear your performance of a minute ago," said Auntie Siobhan with her eyebrow raised. "I've heard more refined fishwives."

So had Mr. Valentine, if only my aunt knew it.

The atmosphere at 'Long Barrow' was charged with apprehension for the next few days. Conversations were few and the usual light-hearted banter around the table at mealtimes had faded to nothing.

Despite our trepidation, when the telephone finally rang and Uncle Conn said:

"And a good afternoon to you too, Niall Valentine," there was an audible release of breath.

Even though we didn't know what was being said, at least the tension had been broken.

"I see, I see…" said uncle who listened for a moment before replacing the receiver.

"Niall has agreed to meet the O'Neills with me at 'Redmile' tomorrow morning,"

WHAT?!

"Oh, and Bridie, seeing she's an O'Neill too."

Auntie left the room before she could say anything she'd regret.

Ten minutes later, from the open door, I watched Cathal mount Ghost and trot off down the lane. Seemed Niall Valentine wasn't the only one needing time for serious thought.

Chapter Thirty-five
Mud

It was pouring with rain when the family fell out of the door the following morning, donning jackets and pulling on rubber boots, The yard was already slippery with mud and liquid excrement.

I looked at the sky. It appeared to carry the Biblical flood: dark grey clouds scudded in a gale-force wind, which blasted raindrops like pennies into my face.

"I'll call Niall," said Uncle Conn. "We can't travel in this."

"No, don't do that," I said. "Neave and I will go. Two delicate little flowers dripping like drowned rats can only add to our cause.

"Aw, c'mon," I encouraged, taking note of Neave's expression. "It's only a bit of water - it won't kill you."

I'd good cause to regret that statement.

Uncle Conn saddled Henry, saying he'd be steadier in the muddy conditions. By this time it didn't matter anyway as we were soaked right down to the skin.

I grinned at Neave.

"Good for the complexion!" I said, which raised a wan smile in return.

It was six miles to 'Redmile' and we hadn't gone more than four, taking our time on the pot-holed, mud-splattered road, before an ominous rumble began in the distance.

Oh shit! Thunder.

Already Henry's eyes were showing white. If it began to lighten, he'd panic.

Before the thought had gone from my head, the whole sky, horizon to horizon was lit by a blinding flash of white, accompanied by a loud crack of thunder. The rain came down even harder.

Henry stood stock-still for a second or two, during which time I tried to rein him in, but I wasn't strong enough, and when the second rumble began he reared throwing us both backwards and bolted for home.

As Neave was holding onto my waist from behind, when we fell I landed on top of her, and actually heard the crack when her arm broke.

But that wasn't the worst of it. When I leapt to my feet, covered in mud from head to foot and screaming her name in terror, Neave wasn't moving. That her left arm was broken was clear by the bone poking through the skin.

In the almighty din of the thunderstorm, I felt for a pulse and put my head to her chest. She was still alive.

I ran my hand through my hair turning this way and that, trying to calm myself enough to think clearly. I couldn't carry her so I'd have to run.

I took off my coat and tucked it round her, being careful not to touch her arm, and ran as if all the hounds of hell were on my tail.

"Please... please help me," I repeated to every angel in heaven and a few below as well. I was still repeating my little prayer and gasping as I collapsed on the doorstep at the Valentine home. The maid who had opened the door ran to fetch Mrs. Valentine, horrified by what she perceived as a mud-covered crazy-woman.

Mr. Valentine himself and Aidan were calming their own animals in the stables but Mrs. Valentine wrapped me in towels and tried to work out what I was yelling about.

"Please help us! We were on our way to see Mr. Valentine when the storm broke and our horse bolted."

I told them about Neave and begged them to send someone to fetch her.

Rosalind ran out into the rain, slipping and sliding, her hem filthy to the knees before she'd covered twenty paces. She dragged her father away and I saw her take his arm, explaining as they ran.

"It'll have to be on foot," he said, throwing on a waxed overcoat, "and I'm afraid you'll need to come with me Bridie. I may not be able to find her."

I was halfway to the lane before he caught me up.

By now tired and out of breath, I reiterated what I'd told his wife and added that her arm was badly broken.

When we found Neave she was semi-conscious but had managed to pull herself a yard or two towards the road with her good arm. It must have been too much because she'd lost consciousness again.

"Have you anything to secure her arm?" asked Mr. Valentine, better heard since the storm was now abating.

I pulled off my belt - it was all I could think of.

"Will this do? It won't be comfortable."

"Neither will this," he said, taking her hand and tugging hard to pull the bone into line again.

Binding her arm with a large pocket handkerchief, he wrapped her in his coat and trying to ignore her screams, ran for home.

I followed as best I could.

In Neave and Cathal's New York there had been abundant running water, but here although Mr. Valentine had managed to pipe it to the yard for the animals, the house still relied on its gas boiler in the wash-house for hot water drawn from a well.

Ah, the luxury of servants! Within a half-hour I was taking a warm bath and wrapping myself in one of Rosalind's robes while she dried and combed out my hair.

"What beautiful hair you have," she said, dragging my head back with the force of her brushing.

When I checked out my appearance in a mirror afterwards, I had to admit she'd done a wonderful job. My clean hair hung in rosy tresses to my waist and smelled sweetly of lavender.

I wrapped the robe tightly round me. Although no-one would have given a hoot in New York, here in old-fashioned Ireland it wouldn't have been considered decent to sit in a room of men dressed as I was.

I was so tired that when I was shown to a comfortable bed, I slept soundly until dawn.

Chapter Thirty-Six
Ghost's History Explained

It must have been about five o'clock and still dark when I was awoken by a flurry of activity outside. I dragged back the heavy velvet curtains and peeped round them at the yard below.

There stood five men, each grim-faced. Uncle Conn, Daniel and Cathal were confronting the Valentines.

I could hear nothing through the closed window of course, but there was a lot of wild gesticulating going on, and they were all talking on top of each other, so I guessed very little was heard by any of them.

At that time in the morning everyone - even the servants - had been woken by the noise, and propriety forgotten were gathered in their robes in the hall.

I arrived about the same time as Rosalind and her mother - both looking as disheveled as me, although Rosalind still managed to resemble a flower unfolding.

"Where's Neave," I breathed. "After yesterday, I don't want them blundering in on her unprepared at this time in the morning. Dan's over- emotional at the best of times, and this isn't one of them - best of times, I mean."

Rosalind grabbed me by the arm and we fled up the stairs where Neave lay pale as an apparition with blue shadows under her eyes. I kissed her forehead and gently shook her awake.

"I just wanted to prepare you for the chaos to come, Honey. Your beloved, his father and your brother are about to charge up the stairs. For your own sake, try to look better."

We managed to hoist her further up the bed, propped her pillows behind her and I pinched her cheeks to try to give her some color.

It was disheartening that so far she hadn't uttered a word. This was going to be a disaster, and there was no way I wasn't going to get the blame.

"You can't walk about like that all day. I'll get you one of my dresses," said Rosalind as we turned to go. "It'll be a bit loose round the waist but we can pin it."

"Least of my worries," I said, chewing my lip and forgetting to thank her.

I looked back at Neave over my shoulder as we reached the door. She'd lifted her head from the pillows and was pinching her own cheeks. I offered a small prayer of thanks. If she was conscious they might think twice about stringing me up.

Dan blundered in and nearly knocked both of us flat in his desperate lunge to get at Neave. He dropped to his knees next to the bed and kissed her hand. Rosalind and I left.

Once I had dressed, Rosalind and I joined the men - minus the family sap - sitting around the dining room table.

Rather than the second Great War I'd been expecting, the conversation was quite civilized and mostly comprised apologies from the Cullen side at having intruded on

Valentine kindness, and reassurances from the Valentines that 'what else would you expect from dear friends'.

Dear friends? I must have missed more of the conversation than I'd thought. How had they gone in two days from murder to best buddies?

Aidan slid into the chair next to mine, held me to his chest and rubbed his face against my hair quite openly. His mother gave him a dirty look, which he ignored.

Cathal interrupted the small-talk by clearing his throat.

"Mr. Valentine, sir - I have a subject to discuss with you which is the reason Neave and I are here. You too, Mr. Cullen because in a way I've been under your roof under false pretenses as well."

He took a deep breath and continued:

"I ask you will please hear me out - some of what I say may not be to your liking.

"I don't come to make excuses for my grandfather. I can't undo what he did, only tell you how sorry I am and try my best to come to some agreement sir, which you will find acceptable in reparation."

"I fail to see how you can do that," chipped in Aidan with a smirk.

They were like chalk and cheese those two - Cathal tall, urbane and distinctly Irish in appearance; Aidan smaller, hot-tempered but friendly, except when challenged.

We were interrupted by Daniel rapping loudly on the door.

"Mr. Valentine, Neave asks if Cathal has come to complete his task, she might be present. She says she helped him every step of the way with the planning, so if any blame is to be attached to his actions she should take her share."

Neave was carried in draped over Dan's arms like the consumptive in 'Camille'.

He made sure she was comfortable in a plush, deep-upholstered armchair and Mrs. Valentine tucked a blanket over her knees.

They were all fussing about her and it was beginning to become tedious. Aidan clearly thought the same. His foot was tapping impatiently against the table leg.

"So what's this reparation for the harm done my family, which killed my grandfather," - *poetic license* - "and near drove us into bankruptcy?" Aidan asked, suspiciously.

Cathal had a way of looking down his nose which was decidedly supercilious, and he could maintain an uncomfortable silence effortlessly. It was an old fashioned concept, but he'd a lifetime's training in command of the O'Neills and just slipped into the manner instinctively.

"Leave us!" Niall said to everyone in the room, and when Aidan made to stay, said firmly. "You too, Aidan - go."

Aidan glared furiously at Cathal as he left.

Everyone left but Niall, brother, sister and me, since Neave refused to let go of my hand.

185

Cathal moved to the window and stood looking towards the stable where a groom had brought Ghost into the sunshine and was attempting to brush dry mud from his fetlocks and hooves, but Ghost was trying to rear, his loathing of grooms once again evident.

"Please excuse me - I'll be back directly. I need to take Ghost from your lad before he gets kicked."

Cathal left at a run.

Daniel was waiting for us, sitting on the stairs in the hall and Cathal grabbed his arm.

"Ghost!" he said. Dan understood at once and fled.

Cathal returned to the dining room where he and Mr. Valentine watched Dan dismiss the groom and calm the panicky horse.

"I raised Ghost from a colt and he is calmer with me than anyone else but Daniel. That lad has a natural way with beasts I've never seen before," said Cathal to Mr. Valentine.

They stood quietly for a few minutes watching Dan, before Mr. Valentine said:

"I take it you didn't come here to discuss your equine, Mr. O'Neill. What's on your mind?"

"The horse, as it happens. Ghost has a lineage you might find of interest."

Neave tightened her grip on my hand, aware of what was coming.

"The mare - which Seamus missed - gave birth to Dempsey's King," Niall drew a deep breath and sat forward in his chair.

"And the other?"

"By the will of God, the other mare survived the journey to Donegal and dropped her colt there. Seamus called him Spirit of Tara and kept him well hidden. Too many questions would be asked of his quality.

"He was given to my father and quickly became his own mount. I helped with his care - his dam died soon after his birth. When my father was killed in the fight for Irish independence, although Spirit of Tara passed to my Uncle Brian, it was on condition I inherited any progeny. Spirit fathered only one colt which I named Pride of Tara, but to me he was always Ghost.

"Well... I'll be damned!" said Niall, dumfounded.

"He was always a headstrong animal and only allowed me on his back, even then reluctantly. It took Daniel to discover his hatred of grooms - I can only assume Ghost had been ill-treated for some considerable time. It's to my shame that I didn't know."

Ghost whickered and tossed his head, reminding Cathal once again of his imminent loss.

"With you permission I need some fresh air Mr. Valentine. Would you allow me a little time alone?"

"Take as much time as you like - I could do with some solitude myself to think things over. Why don't you take Ghost to the ridge - over there," he said gesturing out of the window. "It's a relaxing ride."

Chapter Thirty-seven
Lorelei No More

After Cathal had left and Mr. Valentine had gone to his stables, I persuaded Neave to go back to bed and Rosalind and I kept her company.

As Rosalind smiled and chatted away, I took some time to watch her. She was kind and thoughtful, occasionally rearranging Neave's pillows, or pouring her a glass of water.

Neave was still lethargic but, under Rosalind's ministrations she had begun to smile a little.

When Cathal returned, the meeting resumed, but rather than moving Neave downstairs again, Mr. Valentine had a couple of wing chairs placed in her room and the discussion continued there.

That Cathal was nervous probably wouldn't have been apparent to most, but I had come to know him well..

"By rights sir, Pride of Tara belongs to you. Now Dempsey is gone and he is the last of his line I would like you to have him."

Niall Valentine sat forward in his seat and grasped his chair arms.

"What do you mean, boy? You are giving him to me? Giving...., no payment? Why in God's name would you do that?"

"Both his sire and dam and their progeny should by rights be yours. I can't replace all those lost years but I will make what reparation I can to restore a little of my family's honor. Besides which I could never sell him - there isn't enough money in the world."

Neave burst into tears.

"You can never replace him, my brother. How can you do this?"

No-one was aware Aidan had enter the room until he spoke.

"I'm pleased to hear that, Cathal O'Neill," he turned to his father and said:

"Isn't that the best news, Father? He can be mine since I lost Dempsey to that bastard Doyle. Gelding should calm him."

"Gelding?" said Cathal in disbelief. "He's the last of a line, going back to racing the beach at Laytown in the 1860s!"

"He should be used for breeding. If we are successful, perhaps you can have one of his foals to bring on," said Niall to his son.

Poor Aidan. I could see he was heartbroken. Just for a moment he'd imagined Dempsey's half-brother could make up for his own horse's loss. His father had squashed the dawning optimism flat.

Aidan turned and fled, slamming the door behind him.

Such had been the shock of the offer, all eyes returned to Cathal.

I took his hand in comfort. His face showed the same shell-shock as Uncle Conn's when confronted by the IRA debacle on the quay in Dublin. He was lost in his own mind. He pushed me away, his eyes fixed on Niall Valentine.

"Please, Mr. Valentine. Please don't let him do that."

"Calm yourself, Cathal. Aidan's got a temper on him. He'll come round when he's had time to think."

There was the scream of a furious horse, a loud shout and the clatter of hooves on cobbles.

When we got to him, Danny was standing in the middle of the stable yard, stunned.

"I couldn't stop him, Mr. Valentine. When he mounted, Ghost reared and he took the whip to him. They were both out of control and heading for [1]*na sléibhte fianna"* up above Cordonagh. I couldn't catch them if I tried."

Mr. Valentine took charge. "Tom, Robbie, Cal….," he called his grooms to him, "Saddle the three fastest. Conn, Daniel, Cathal, lend a hand and we'll see if we can't corner him, although it'll be well-nigh impossible on open moorland. It's soft underfoot up there. Ghost could come to harm."

"I'm coming too," I said, slinging the first available saddle across the first available mount and tightening the girth.

This was my Aidan, and Lorelei was coming to the rescue. Except I arrived five minutes after everyone else

But as it turned out, Ghost wasn't the one harmed.

[1] The wild fells

They were finally found on the moorland heights. Ghost was calmly cropping the short grass next to a rocky outcrop, his reins hanging loose.

Aidan lay face down on the earth, blood in his hair, his arms thrown outwards, his body lifeless.

Cathal went to examine Ghost and ran expert hands over each of his legs, checking for damage.

"Aidan banged his head when he fell," said Cathal, who was more concerned with Ghost's welfare.

When he was quite satisfied Ghost was uninjured, he mounted, leaving Niall, Conn and Dan to deal with Aidan.

"I'll go get a stretcher," he said, turning Ghost about and walking him down the slope.

When Aidan was slow to regain consciousness, Cathal rode to Wicklow town to fetch back a doctor who flashed a light in Aidan's eyes, and when that woke him sufficiently - which it did eventually - made him follow his finger back and forth.

Aidan, he announced, was suffering from concussion from the blow to the head and needed a few days bed rest.

He then snapped shut his bag, put on his hat and got into his automobile cursing the country roads, and went home to his dinner.

Rosalind ladled warm soup into her brother's mouth, adjusted the bandage around his head, and I held the bowl to his chin as he vomited the food back up.

.

The following morning Aidan was dead.

Chapter Thirty-eight
Lorelei's Beau Bites the Dust

Rosalind it was who had discovered his body lying rigid when she went to awaken him with breakfast.

She'd been to see Neave first. She was so much better that when Rosalind returned to the kitchen to retrieve Aidan's meal, she was humming happily to herself. She smiled at the thoughtfulness of the kitchen staff, who had arranged a small bunch of wildflowers on the tray.

I was seated in the sunroom with Eefa Valentine who was chatting away to me as she poured tea into delicate china cups from a matching pot.

I gazed inattentively out of the window thinking of Aidan and wondering if I hadn't after all been swayed into this romance by a quick feel in the stable at 'Long Barrow' and being called Lorelei.

The four men - Danny, Cathal, Uncle Conn and Mr. Valentine - were long since in the stables checking out the horses they'd ridden so hard across the moors the day before.

Mrs. Valentine leapt to her feet at Rosalind's ear-shattering scream.

I took the stairs three at a time, with Eefa doing her best to keep up.

Rosalind had put the tray on Aidan's nightstand and bent to shake him awake.

To me at least it was apparent he was dead. His eyes were half open and when I tried to raise his hand to feel for a pulse he was as stiff as a board..

I herded them all back to the sunroom. and splashed a bit of tea into some cups, told them to use plenty of sugar and bolted for the stables.

The only person there was Uncle Conn.

I was so het up and out of breath from running, at first I couldn't string two words together and stood hands on knees drawing in great lungfuls of air. When I was able, I dragged Uncle Conn out of sight of the house and blurted out:

"Aidan's dead…" followed by: "What do I do?"

Not exactly the best way to break the news..

Once he got over the shock, my uncle took me by the shoulders and yelled in my face:

"WHATT! Are you sure?"

People say the daftest things under duress.

When I didn't respond, he told me to stay put while he went to speak to Mr. Valentine. I should have been weeping for Aidan, but in reality my tears were relief at not having to confront his father.

I'd heard the word 'keening' before but I'd never appreciated its true meaning until I followed Niall Valentine into Aidan's room.

Eefa was sobbing into the bedcovers by Aidan's hand and Rosalind, tears streaming down her own face, had pulled up a chair and was trying to persuade her mother into it.

Niall was not so gentle. He lifted his wife under the armpits, deposited her in the chair and began to check his son was indeed dead - pointless really when it was so apparent.

Uncle Conn rode to 'Long Barrow' and returned with his car so we could all take Neave home, There was no place for any of us at 'Redmile'.

Chapter Thirty-nine
Who is Rosalind?

The next we heard from the Valentines was an invitation to Aidan's wake. Unlike Uncle Brian's, this was a proper one, held in the church hall in Cordonagh. Neave and Cathal were excluded which came as no surprise.

Lots of alcohol was provided and later added to.

As the Valentines were viewed as local aristocracy, the wake was lavish, and Aidan's body was laid out in a silk-lined casket looking pale, despite the dusting of powder the undertaker had applied to his face.

As the evening wore on and more drink was consumed, there was impromptu dancing and singing, wild and raucous as only the Irish know how.

Ronan played his drum with gusto although his mother kept him well away from the liquor. He was accompanied by a fiddler, someone turned up with an Irish harp and there were hearty, slurred choruses of 'Danny Boy' and 'Wild Rover'.

Women who hardly left their door stoops danced in rings with sweaty farmers from the distant hills - nobody missed a good wake.

Halfway through the evening, Father Lynch appeared, whisky in hand, to comfort the bereaved and tell them of the promise of Paradise for their son, a good Catholic lad.

Once he'd gone, Auntie Siobhan questioned the priest's adherence to the Good Book, telling her devout husband loud and often 'the Holy Joe' should have been put down at birth. Everyone prayed the whisky wouldn't loosen her tongue and there was an audible sigh of relief when the priest left the wake.

I threaded my way through the heaving throng to look at Aidan. At least they hadn't propped him up in a chair as was often done.

With a little difficulty, I loosened the cross he had given me as a love token from around my neck and tucked it beneath his folded hands. He could take a little bit of his Lorelei to the grave.

When the heat and noise became overpowering, I went outdoors to sit on the church wall. There I found Rosheen, quietly gazing where the mountains should have been but for the dark.

She was deep in thought and jumped when I sat next to her. To that point she hadn't shown emotion but now she had a sympathetic listener, the whole story of herself and Aidan tumbled out.

She'd adored him all her life she said and showed me a gold cross he'd given her with 'Freyja' engraved upon it. It was identical to my own but for the inscription.

"She was the redhaired goddess of the Germans," she whispered.

Well - the bastard! And a goddess whereas I was merely a maiden.

"I didn't believe it when everyone said he was promised to you. That couldn't have been true since he was just awaiting the right time to talk to Da for me."

"But you were at the dance when he declared himself before the whole village!"

"Humph! That was the whisky talking. Dan said so himself."

'There's none so blind as those who just will *not* see' as the saying goes.

It would serve no purpose arguing with her, so I left her to her dreams and went back inside. It would have come to nothing with me anyway - I'd already been having second thoughts. Perhaps he was just hedging his bets.

Mr. Valentine was 'hosting' the wake, so was obliged to shake hands with all and sundry as they left.

Mrs. Valentine just sobbed into a lace handkerchief doused in lavender water. Rosalind sat beside her, every so often patting her hand, She looked absolutely exhausted. She'd just had three days of singlehandedly caring for the sick and bereaved and she could hardly stand up.

"I'm taking Rosalind home," I announced to her parents, "She's completely spent. You've already enough on your hands. I'll take care of her."

I helped Rosalind prepare for bed - her sadness had tired her out and the noise and heat had just been too much for her.

The business was only half over - tomorrow was her brother's funeral and another round of putting her own grief to one side while she attended to others.

While she washed and climbed into bed, I made her some warm milk and sat with her while she drank it.

"Don't be angry, Rosalind but there's a question I've been meaning to ask. If you consider it none of my business, I apologize."

She encouraged me to continue.

"You look like someone I've seen before but try as I might I just can't put my finger on who.

"You have the look of your father about you as Aidan has - sorry, had," I said scarlet-faced, "but that's all."

"It's never spoken about," she said quietly, "but for some time I've wondered if Mama is my mother at all. I've no reason for thinking that - no-one has ever said anything to me directly. It's just little things - my eyes are blue, hers are hazel, her hair is darkish brown, mine is not quite blonde but near enough. And our build is totally different - she's tall and elegant and I'm….. "she put her head on one side in thought, "I suppose you could call me unremarkable."

I couldn't believe she was saying this. She was young, perhaps mid-twenties, with honey-colored hair so soft no clip would hold it, a slender frame and gentle manner which invited confidences.

Chapter Forty
After the Funer

The funeral was surprisingly understated. There's one thing about a wake - which is the point I suppose - the following day everyone is so knackered there's little desire to weep and wail.

The exception is naturally the immediate family which included my friend Rosalind. As usual she was doing her best to be all things to all people - supplying her mother with handkerchiefs and putting her hand consolingly through her father's arm.

She excelled at hymns, though. I was surprised to hear she had a beautiful contralto voice, which soared effortlessly over the rest of the congregation's. It wasn't one of those deafening, pushy 'old ladies' voices, but comforting and spiritual. She turned 'Be Thou My Vision' into a song of redemption for everyone there.

With the exception of Dan, to whom Aidan had been like a brother, the Cullens didn't attend the interment, considering it a family affair. The following day, we all went to put flowers on the grave. I never saw Rosheen shed more than a tear or two before. Only I knew why she was inconsolable, although I guess her mother had her own suspicions.

After a week during which auntie had refused to allow Uncle Conn to telephone, saying they'd still be grieving, I

...ted to see Rosalind who was again confined to the ...ouse.

Her father would never allow her to attend social events, other than those held at her home which were few. Indeed, I'd never even seen her in Cordonagh.

Niall Valentine never behaved that way with his son, which was puzzling for someone like me, who could never quash her curiosity.

I found Rosalind reading a book in the sun room.

"Would you like to take a trip to Dublin with me? Uncle and Dan are going next week. They'll be staying overnight and back the following morning. "It'd be fun - we can go shopping and eat in a restaurant. Dan can act as chaperone."

I hooted with laughter at the thought of Dan chaperoning anyone. I could bully him into submission on my own. Two of us would scare him to death.

"I don't think Papa will allow it. I've stopped asking - the answer is always the same," she said with resignation.

But strange to say, this time he did allow it. Perhaps it was the trauma of her brother's death or he considered the company of another girl a sufficient safety barrier, I don't know. Perhaps it was simply to get her away from her mother who was still walking round the house wringing her hands like Lady MacBeth.

We spent some time throwing a ball on the grass for her dog until it splashed into the carp pond and left one of the fish floundering on the colored tiles of the surround, and the dog covered in waterweed. I picked up the slimy fish with distaste and threw it back into the water.

While Rosalind dashed her dog into the house for a towel I was left alone to reflect upon the happenings of the past few weeks. One death, one near-death and a love affair - more downs than ups.

The books I'd brought with me from 'Túr Capaill' as a gift for Molly were still at the bottom of the suitcase under my bed, to that point completely forgotten.

Rosalind returned without the dog and sat next to me on the lawn. She would want to know about her grandfather's message. I hoped it might cheer her and give her something else to think about.

"There was something I had to tell you about - but with all the recent happenings I'd quite forgotten. While I was noseying around at the Tower before Cathal's uncle died I came across an old library created by Seamus's mother.

"In it I found a copy of "Pride and Prejudice" in three volumes.

"Inside the second volume was an inscription which read... if I remember aright. Darn I've forgotten the exact words -

well, words to the effect of an affectionate dedication from Edmond Valentine to a 'Kitty'"

"Who's Kitty?" asked Rosalind.

"Well, that's the interesting bit," I confided in a whisper. "She was Seamus's first wife - at least she's the only Kitty Neave and Cathal know of in their family. She was christened Caroline but was nicknamed Kitty. You can't know any more than I do if you don't know who Kitty is," I added, disappointed.

"I don't, but I'll search the house and see if I can come up with anything," Rosalind paused. "You don't suppose this could be at the root of the conflict between the Valentines and the O'Neills, do you?"

"Might be something to do with your incarceration as well," I mused. "That's unusual, too."

Chapter Forty-one
A Parting and a Declaration

While Rosalind and I had been living the high life in Dublin, Cathal had gone to see Mr. Valentine again.

He was in something of a quandary since his sacrifice to the cause of the Valentine/O'Neill feud was now not so straightforward.

Aidan had been killed in a fall from Cathal's beloved horse, his beautiful Ghost, his Pride of Tara, his priceless piece of Irish equine history.

He wondered if Mr. Valentine would take into account that the fall was entirely Aidan's own fault as Dan could verify. Even though he was well within his rights to have the horse destroyed because his son had been killed, if one of Ghost's legs had been broken there would have been no choice. Niall would have had to dole out the same treatment as Joe Doyle had to Dempsey. Damaging Cathal's beloved horse may perhaps have been Aidan's intention.

Aidan sure had taken a dislike to Cathal.

When we returned after our trip, Rosalind's father told her of Cathal's visit.

He had been in a meeting with his stable master, so Cathal was left to kick his heels in the hall and had filled in the time by idly examining the pictures on the wall.

When Niall came out of his office, it was to find Cathal deep in thought before a large watercolor of a lovely young woman with a gentle face and hair twisted into a soft bun on top of her head. It was the only modern painting in the hall and had always been a particular favorite of Niall's who'd found her direct smile both disconcerting and enchanting. It seemed it had struck Cathal the same way.

"Such beauty. Is she a family member? I'm sorry sir - that's none of my business, and in any case she was not the purpose of my visit."

His expression became somber.

"In view of what has happened, I don't suppose Ghost will be a welcome gift."

He went on to offer his condolences and to let Mr. Valentine know he would be returning to 'Túr Capaill' as soon as courtesy to the Cullen's would permit. He would be taking Ghost with him.

Then he left, shutting the door quietly behind him.

"Damn, I like that young man," murmured Niall Valentine to himself.

Once Rosalind had returned home, and uncle, Dan and I were back at 'Long Barrow', auntie set to to prepare a feast.

If Mr. Valentine didn't understand Aidan was to blame for his own death, then Aunt Siobhan was determined the whole neighborhood would know she did.

Sean had killed a couple of capons which auntie had plucked and gutted - sadly not the awful Boru who was too old, too tough and seemingly immortal.

Rosheen was noticeable by her absence and I saw her mother, grim-faced, glance every so often at her empty chair at the table.

Everyone had their own place and their own tasks to perform. Neave was doing her best to keep up but eventually auntie told her to sit down. Her broken arm was getting in the way.

Cathal left the announcement of his departure until after the meal, by which time Rosheen had reappeared. Auntie understood his intentions and said he was welcome under her roof any time he was passing.

'Not often,' I thought to myself, 'seeing that he lived close on a hundred and fifty miles away.'

I thought back to when I left my family in Dungannon Road. Best thing I ever did, but I doubted my two friends would feel the same.

Although Cathal and his sister would always be close, Daniel was now the center of Neave's life and she had inherited the entire 'Long Barrow' family. Rosie admitted to quite liking her, so she should do well, but Cathal looked sad and abandoned.

Therefore, when he went missing later that evening, I knew where to find him. He'd be in his go-to place in times of stress - Ghost's stall.

Whereas when his uncle had died Cathal was distraught, thinking he was in some way to blame, this time he was knocking hell out of a saddle with a brush prior to polishing it. Ghost was looking nervous so things must have been bad.

He glowered at me, almost snarled, and went back to his work.

"Well... er...,"

Far from helpful, but it's difficult to hold a conversation with someone who so clearly wishes you were somewhere else. I'd try again and if there was still no response, I'd go and swill out the yard.

"Look," he said with an obvious attempt at patience which wouldn't last long. "Leave me the fuck alone, Bridie. I'm in no mood for your interference."

My WHAT! Sonofabitch!

"Now just a minute, you jumped up bastard! I may not be the most sensitive person in the world, but at least I'm not an arrogant, no-good excuse for an aristocrat like you, so I don't need to be - interfering that is! Go to hell."

I turned to march off for my bucket and brush, and in one movement he'd stood, turned me round and was kissing me passionately.

I must admit it was very nice. He'd to almost lift me off my feet to reach my lips and, my Lord, he could kiss. Made Aidan look like an amateur.

'Oh, please, please, please,' I prayed. 'Don't let this be a one-off.'

Cathal deposited me on top of Ghost's manger and rested his face against my shoulder, drained by the days happenings.

He hugged and kissed me again, this time with affection rather than lust. If in that moment he'd asked me to marry him, I'd have asked 'when?'.

After a few minutes when he'd had time to calm down he apologized.

"I'm sorry Bridie - that wasn't the behavior of a gentleman."

I was reminded of Uncle Conn's instructions to Dan about gentlemanly behavior on the voyage to New York when we'd to share a cabin. That wouldn't do at all.

"Oh no you don't!" I said, having nothing of the lady about me and kissed him back with enthusiasm.

He leaped to his feet red in the face and panting. After one or two long deep breaths and swilling his face round with cold water from Ghost's bucket he said:

"If you're leading me on Bridie, please stop. I'm finding it difficult to let go even though I know you were meant for Aidan. Please forgive me."

"Aidan who?" I said and kissed him again.

Chapter Forty-two
A Surprise for Dan and Neave

Since it was less than a month since Aidan's death, this sudden *volte face* had to be temporarily concealed or both our situations might be precarious, on that we were agreed.

The following day Neave helped Daniel lead the horses to pasture, and as it was the kind of gloriously breezy day when cloud shadows scudded across the mountain sides, I was allowed to go with them in place of Uncle Conn.

Cathal was left with my uncle, talking horses. Uncle had always fancied raising his own thoroughbreds. He didn't want to race them. Like Niall Valentine he merely wanted to breed them and raise the foals for sale.

He asked Cathal if Niall would sell him a couple of fine brood mares, would he be willing to allow Ghost to service them - for a generous fee of course.

It wasn't a deep conversation - more exploratory than anything else - but something for them both to think about.

After they'd eaten lunch, uncle was in an expansive frame of mind and gave Cathal the afternoon off. Rather than being honored guests, he and his sister had become extra labor - in short they'd been adopted as honorary Cullens, so Cathal headed up to the pasture to spend time with Neave. But he also had another purpose in mind.

This was the first time he'd had the chance to speak privately to us - apart from our 'fandango' in the stables when speaking wasn't exactly a priority.

He surprised me - and everyone else - by hugging me and kissing me lightly on the lips. Everyone went red except Cathal who was the only one not amazed.

"Jesus, Mary and Joseph!...," exclaimed Danny, which more or less covered the situation.

Cathal described the portrait he'd seen at 'Redmile'.

"She was a young woman, perhaps in her early twenties. She had light brown hair pinned on top of her head and a pointy chin," he paused and added, "She stared straight at you, it was a bit disconcerting."

As this was a typical man's description of a pretty woman I began to translate it into female terms.

'Young. Fine honey-colored hair tied into a soft bun atop her head and a heart-shaped face.'

"Did she have a mouth shaped like this?"

I drew the shape of a 'cupid's bow' in the air. He agreed.

"THE WOMAN IN THE PAINTING AT 'TUR CAPAILL'," Neave and I yelled at the same time.

"If that's right, it's odd there should be likenesses of her at 'Túr Capaill' and 'Redmile', when the families were daggers drawn," mused Cathal. "But I have to admit there is a resemblance."

"Perhaps she's the reason they *were* at daggers drawn," said Neave, dreamily.

Her flights of fancy certainly made up for her fiancé's total lack of imagination.

"Of course, there's another link between the Valentines and O'Neills," I pondered aloud. "The dedication I found in a book. What was it again? Something about faithfulness…,"

"To my most beloved Kitty, Yours ever in true fidelity, Edmond Valentine," trotted out my starry-eyed friend without a pause.

"Perhaps the portraits were both of Kitty O'Neill - Seamus's wife," said Danny who's grasp of the situation seemed to be lagging behind. "A bit of fornication? It must have made Seamus pretty mad if Edmond was having a roll in the hay with his wife."

"Not much fidelity going on," I snorted, making Neave laugh.

"To summarize," said Cathal, trying to pull the conversation back on track, "we've two portraits, seemingly of the same woman - one in Wicklow and one a hundred and fifty miles away in Donegal. She appears to be connected to both the O'Neills and the Valentines. She could be the woman mentioned in the Bible as Caroline Mickley. Neave believes her to be nicknamed Kitty and to be our grandfather's first wife. Yet the dedication in the book is by Rosalind's grandfather, Edmond Valentine."

"I mentioned the book dedication," I told them, "but Rosalind doesn't know about the Donegal painting."

"Did you notice Rosalind has a look of the portrait at 'Túr Capaill'," said Neave. "She resembles Edmond in the nose and eyes but her mouth is more like the girl in the portrait."

"Yes," said Cathal. "At first I did take the portrait for Rosalind, but it isn't."

Should I tell them about Rosalind's confidence? That she had wondered about her relationship to Eefa Valentine? I decided to keep that to myself, for the time being at least.

Chapter Forty-three
Raguel's Double Surprise

"Complete change of subject," said Cathal. "I've told Mr. Valentine and your uncle I intend returning to Donegal. Ghost will no longer be wanted I think, so there's nothing to keep me."

The look of relief which crossed his face was almost comical.

WHAT! I'd be damned if this was going to happen twice. I put my full weight down on Cathal's foot. When he grunted in pain, Neave saw and grinned.

"Told you he'd no staying power," she said, referring to the day the four of us first met.

He gave her a blank stare, got down on one knee and took a small red velvet box from his pocket.

"I've been carrying this around since we left 'Túr Capaill'," he said, opening it to show the sparkliest bit of jewelry I'd ever seen - even better than anything in the window of Cartier in New York.

"I love your Bridie O'Neill - please say you'll be my wife."

That beat Lorelei hands down.

Before I could say anything and as if she'd read my mind, Neave chimed in:

"It's a Cartier. It belonged to our mother."

Cathal glared at her to be silent.

"Well... will you?" Cathal asked, rising from his knees and looking a bit put out by my silence. In truth, I was so goddam flummoxed I was incapable of speech.

"Well, at least she didn't say no," observed Dan.

"Well... will you or not?" groused my future husband.

Words were not enough. I jumped into his arms and kissed him fervidly.

"I'll take that as a yes," he whispered against my cheek.

"You do realize you'll have to do a repeat performance for Ma," said Danny. "She'll be livid if she thinks someone knows before she does."

Dinner that evening was a quiet affair until Cathal repeated his proposal - then all hell broke loose.

"That's my daughter you're talking about - you'd better be serious or I hope the O'Neill clan have life insurance," threatened my aunt.

"She's not your daughter," corrected Rosheen.

"As much as you are, my girl - make no mistake," replied her mother.

Cathal did the knee bit again and I saw Neave and Daniel exchange a secret smile.

"Oh well," said Dan to Neave with no graciousness at all, "I suppose you'd better have this."

He opened a small box containing a beautiful square-cut diamond ring. Neave's eyes opened wide and, like I'd been, she was speechless.

"Got it in Dublin. It can't come as a shock," said Dan, "I did propose."

When had he become so laconic? He used to be earnest, eager to please. He was no longer a boy, I supposed.

"By the Archangel Raguel," said Uncle Conn. "It's a double celebration we have!"

"Angel of Love," whispered Sean in my ear.

Auntie's warning the Valentines might be offended by the shortness of time since their son's death, were drowned out by the din of cheers, scraping chairs and backslaps of congratulations. In the end she shrugged and joined in.

Daniel took it in good part - he'd grown up with this family and understood their moods. Cathal looked amazed and embarrassed, and blushed.

Rosie brought out two bottles of her father's whisky then went to the still room for ginger beer for the young ones, and a real Irish party ensued.

Later, when the pandemonium had died down, the kids were in bed and my aunt and uncle were cuddling by the fireside, Cathal tugged me out back, lifted me onto the water-barrel lid and kissed me until both our bodies hummed.

Next I knew we were in the hay-loft, all sense and reason out of the window, sharing more pleasure than I could ever have imagined.

Chapter Forty-four
A Hand-Fasting.

Out of respect for my aunt and uncle, Cathal and I parted reluctantly. He with Daniel, who wasn't stupid enough to risk his mother's wrath again, went back to the stables and Neave and I tried to sleep in the house.

The following morning over breakfast, something was certainly eating at Cathal.

"I can't get married here," he said turning to me. "I'm sorry Bridie - It's just not possible."

The silence was deafening, everyone waiting for the explosion sure to come.

When he kissed me softly on the lips and hugged me I gave a sigh of relief. He wasn't dumping me.

"As a chief of my clan, I'm obliged to marry at 'Túr Capaill'. At least that's the tradition. It wouldn't be taken kindly if I didn't, especially as recently I've spent so much time away.

"I also have work I've been delaying and my business manager is beginning to panic. He's even taken to wiring me lately. So it might even be that a trip to New York is on the cards at some point."

I couldn't see how this was relevant.

"But if Dan and Neave marry soon, I would like to stay for the wedding. If you'll have me," he pleaded, looking at Aunt Siobhan for permission.

"I don't see how we can wed if my best man's across the country in Donegal - or across the world in New York," said Dan. Neave threw her arms around his neck in delight.

"Right," said Auntie Siobhan, "I'll get on it then."

She bustled from the table and I heard her yell like a foghorn down the telephone:

"Father Lynch, get your cassock on. There's going to be a wedding - first free date in your book."

Cathal jumped from the table and got to her just as her finger touched the dial.

"If that's Mrs. Valentine, please don't call. I have to go over myself and if she's still grieving I don't want to bother her any more than necessary. Even so, I told Mr. Valentine I'd be leaving and, with his agreement taking Ghost back to Donegal. If I'm to be delayed, I at least owe him the courtesy of telling him why."

"Don't lose this one," Uncle Conn said to me. "He's worth keeping."

I confess I worried about Mr. Valentine taking a shotgun to him or Ghost, but Cathal explained that although their last meeting wasn't friendly, it was at least cordial and they had parted on speaking terms. The same couldn't be said of Mrs. Valentine, however.

"Oh never mind her," huffed auntie. I'll take care of that."

Rosheen rode to 'Redmile' with Cathal to explain recent events.

They took ages to come back, and just as I was beginning to suspect Niall Valentine had indeed pummeled Cathal to a pulp, the pair of them rounded a bend in the lane.

Neave and I were waiting sitting on the five-bar gate. She was fine but I was trying my best to look unconcerned when in actual fact I was shaking.

"Oh, don't be such a sap," snapped Rosie, who'd climbed over the gate beside us. "Look, he's still alive - well, mostly," she added looking at his clenched teeth.

Cathal dismounted then went to lift Rosheen down, but she was already half way to the door, throwing her reins to Rosie, who was left outside fuming, while the four of us put auntie out of her misery.

"Sit," said Aunt Siobhan.

Rosheen began to tell the tale only to be ordered to hold her tongue.

"Mr. Valentine was very kind and thanked me for explaining the situation...." began Cathal.

"I suppose he was," said auntie. "Courtesy is in his nature. All these ups and downs won't sit well with him at all."

"I'm so relieved he's not angry," breathed Neave. "I so wanted Rosalind to be one of my bridesmaids."

Two of the four of us - Dan and me - burst out laughing.

"She hasn't been allowed out of the house in years," I explained.

"Why?" asked Neave. "She came to Aidan's funeral."

"Yes, so she did," said auntie thoughtfully. "Now there's a thing,"

The arrangements became organized chaos conducted by Auntie Siobhan.

It began when she shipped in Mrs. Cormack from Wicklow with all her assistants to measure, cut patterns and stitch for bride and bridesmaids.

Auntie called Eefa Valentine who now there was a wedding on the cards, had forgotten all hostilities - so much so that Dan was exiled to 'Redmile' for the duration of the preparations, riding the eight miles to the pastures daily. Craig took over his chores at 'Long Barrow' farm while Dan lent Mr. Valentine a hand.

As with all girls, Neave knew precisely what she wanted for a wedding gown. It was a long, dropped waist 'flapper' type affair entirely covered in Limerick lace, with a trailing veil edged in the same design of shamrocks and horseshoes.

When I suggested Rosheen, Rosie and I would take care of the headdresses and bouquets, Neave jumped up and down with glee.

"Good job you're not dead on the hills," said auntie.

If anything, Rosalind was more delighted than the bride when her father allowed her to accept Neave's offer.

With the exception of her brother's funeral she hadn't been outside the confines of 'Redmile' since her childhood. She was a gentle, patient person and not given to complaining, but I could tell she was desperately lonely. It was as if she'd accepted she would never be allowed to have a day like Neave's, she would never find a man to love her. How could she? She never met any.

What was wrong with her father that he incarcerated her? Perhaps now she was his only child he might relent.

She *was* permitted to come to 'Long Barrow' for fittings but her mother was nimble-fingered and the sewing was completed at home.

There were four bridesmaids - Rosheen, Rosalind, Rosie and I.

The Wedding Day dawned bright and beautiful with just enough breeze to lift the bride's veil and flutter it down again. The bridesmaids, clad in the palest of pale green silk, were crowned with coral-hued roses, the bride adorned with damask roses of cream, intertwined with myrtle for luck,

As the bride left 'Long Barrow' for the flower-bedecked church, far distant as to be almost an echo, a cuckoo sang glad tidings.

I hardly recognized Daniel when he arrived in a kilt of blue and green Cullen tartan, with his hair tidy and brushed to a shine. Neave was such a lucky girl, for as fine as he looked, his heart was kind and his spirit generous.

But my eyes were all for my future husband who stood tall, straight and serious at his side.

Irish weddings have their odd side. Some traditions are carried out throughout Ireland whereas some are local. The first Neave knew - the second came as something of a surprise.

Instead of Mass - probably because Aunt Siobhan couldn't stand the priest and was paying the bill, the ancient ceremony of handfasting was performed. The bride and groom were tied at the wrist with ribbon, to signify their commitment to each other. Uncle Conn told me that was a female excuse and really it was to hamper the groom's sprint for freedom.

After the reception, Siobhan crumbled a bit of wedding cake over Neave's head. That apparently symbolized good feeling between a new bride and her mother-in-law. It seemed a bit of a dangerous way of going about things to me, especially when Rosie joined in.

The Valentines should still have been in mourning and I suppose they might have been, but the celebration spread like ripples in a pool and everyone was sucked in, including Niall and Eefa.

Rosalind, quite unused to such enthusiastic celebration, stood away from the crowd until Neave and I pulled her forward, and included her in the conversation. Before long she was smiling and talking and for the first time getting to know her neighbors.

I prayed to St Agnes her father would be kind to her.

Chapter Forty-five
'Túr Capaill' Arrivals and a Wedding

After a week's preparation for the journey, the four of us set off on horseback to Donegal for our own wedding. Aunt and Uncle, Rosheen, Molly, Ronan and Rosie were to follow a week later travelling from Dublin to Strabane on the train..

Uncle and Mr. Valentine had agreed that the 'Redmile' stable master would run 'Long Barrow' for the couple of weeks he proposed being away. Sean and Craig offered to stay behind to help as needed. Of course I was devastated my brothers wouldn't be there but understood it could be no other way.

I also learned from Cathal that Jonathan Grainger was travelling to Ireland to conclude any outstanding business, and free him to give his entire and uninterrupted attention to his wife for a few weeks.

We beat the Cullens to 'Túr Capaill' by two whole days, so had some time to recuperate. Jonathan had also arrived and was spending time settling into a staff suite to the rear of the house.

"Cara's going to faint when she sees the extra work," said Neave. "I'll have her arrange help from the village but in the meantime we'll have to pitch in I'm afraid."

By the end of the day our rooms were prepared, and Uncle Conn and Dan shared a moment's amusement at the names. They could both recite the list of Derby winners by heart.

The following morning as the sun streamed through the turret windows, a car rolled up the drive with Jon Grainger at the wheel.

To my utter delight, out climbed Niall and Eefa Valentine and my lovely Rosalind, who was looking around her in wonder.

Only Cathal had known they were coming. He knew how much I wanted Rosalind with me on my wedding day, so he had spoken at length to Niall on the telephone without my knowledge, saying I would be upset and offended if he allowed Rosalind to attend Neave's wedding but not mine.

Cathal was relieved that Mr. Valentine didn't mention the obvious fact that Cordonagh was only a few miles down the road from 'Redmile' and the journey could be covered at a trot in an hour, whereas 'Túr Capaill' was a hundred and fifty miles of uncomfortable train journey. I thought that showed generosity of spirit and boded well for Rosalind's future.

I ran down the three stone steps from the front door and hugged her..

"Oh Rosalind I am so, SO delighted to see you."

"Welcome to the lovely Horse Tower," smiled Neave.

"**Caraaaa!** Bowline and St Brendan!" she shouted, and to her guests: You must be exhausted. Come into the sitting room.

"**Marthaaa!** Break out the Jamesons, soda water and ice and one, two…..and eleven glasses!"

"None of the drink for Molly, Rosie and Ronan of course." auntie was quick to add when they looked optimistic.

"Not for Rosalind and me," said Eefa.

"No, 'course not. **Marthaaa!** Fetch some lemonade from the stillroom - and a pot of tea for Mrs. Valentine."

It was a wonder those girls weren't deaf.

Rosalind had never seen this version of Neave before. In Wicklow, circumstances had made her appear reserved. Here, she was at home and her usual cheery self. Plus she had her Daniel beside her.

Rosalind was slowly being drawn into the lives of the Cullens and O'Neills and at first tentative and shy, she slowly began to unfurl. It was a delight to watch.

After breakfast next morning and while the Valentines were settling in, Neave and Daniel took Aunt Siobhan, Uncle Conn and Rosheen to walk the couple of miles to the south pasture.

After Cathal had set up his own ivory and ebony chessboard for Molly and Ronan and threatened Rosie in no uncertain terms of what he'd do if she broke anything, he and Jon disappeared to the stables.

That left me.

I went to my room and took out the books I still hadn't given to Molly and looked again at the dedication.

I traced my finger over Edmond's signature. It had the formal flow of an educated man. We'd been so taken up with talk of Kitty, no-one had even thought to examine his part in the drama. Perhaps Rosalind knew more.

She had cast doubt on her parentage. Was she right, and if Eefa wasn't her mother, who was?

I also needed to examine what else I knew of Edmond Valentine.

He must have been older than Kitty. Had he been married when he met her?

He must also have been a successful business man. He owned a large stud and was a breeder of thoroughbreds of exceptional quality, or at least had been until Seamus intervened.

I knew he had debts he was unable to repay. Why?

His son, Niall, was no longer a child when he knew Kitty but deeply immersed in his father's business, so much so he was able to help him rebuild the stud after Seamus's malice had ruined his family.

There were so many questions and not enough answers.

When my head began to ache and I was getting nowhere fast, I went to the stables to see Cathal. Our time together had been virtually non-existent on the road.

I'd forgotten about Jonathan, so was surprised when I saw him walking Ghost round the stable yard while Cathal, squatting down, was concentrating on checking his gait.

He got to his feet and nodded tersely to Jon who led Ghost back to his stall.

Once we were alone, Cathal disregarded the whole world and kissed me ardently.

"I missed you," he whispered.

He took my hand and placed his lips gently upon his mother's, now my own engagement ring.

Jon coughed loudly to attract Cathal's attention. I was very gratified to see my beloved looking annoyed at the interruption.

"Yes... yes... what is it? I'm busy."

"I can see that," said Jon, grinning ear to ear. "Never thought I'd see the sight but I'm delighted you finally put a halter on him - Bridget, isn't it? He might be a bit less difficult for the rest of us to deal with now."

"Bridie." I said.

"Ah, Bridie - yes, I remember."

"If you do you'll be one of the few."

Our wedding was the major subject of discussion, naturally, to the point where when we girls were getting into ours stride on the subject, the men would find it convenient to sit outside and smoke.

Slowly as it became *really* tedious, some of the ladies would join them too. That included the bride. Cathal, who liked American cigarettes, had a box full of packs stashed in Neave's parlor. Neave I knew smoked like a chimney as was *de rigueur* in 1920s New York.

In the end, auntie and uncle and the Valentines were the only ones taking tea in the sitting room.

The rest of us sat out on the doorsteps if the weather was clement, or well away from the straw in the stables if it wasn't.

My wedding would be a damn sight easier than Neave's to organize. I could call on the entire Donegal O'Neill clan for support.

Telling tales of Irish weddings tends to get tedious, since all Catholic weddings with a Mass are pretty much the same. Many, like Neave and Danny's are made truly Irish by their additional idiosyncrasies.

Suffice to say, I walked down the aisle in the wedding dress and veil of my fiancé's mother, which being entirely composed of needlepoint lace was the most glorious thing I'd ever seen.

Neave, Rosheen, Rosalind and Rosie were resplendent and rustling in taffeta. It was the first time in her entire life Rosie behaved with decorum without being threatened.

The groom was a complete knockout in an O'Neill tartan kilt and fitted jacket, which looked spectacular with his red hair. And I'd thought Neave was lucky!

Unlike Danny and Neave, Cathal's rank required a proper Mass so it was a perfect day of lace, flowers, friends and relatives - a perfect day except for the bloody piper.

Chapter Forty-six
Niall Valentine's Tale

The four of us had decided to honeymoon in New York, partly so my new husband, Dan and Jonathan could disappear to Kentucky to check out Cathal's stud near Lexington.

Neave, who sighed with boredom at the mere mention of horses, would want to trip the light fantastic at various clubs in New York. It went without saying the two of us would be staying in the house on Byrne Avenue for a while.

But that was yet some time away as Cathal and Jonathan had much outstanding business to take care of in Ireland.

A couple of days after the wedding, Mr. Valentine cornered Cathal in his office.

"Now you will be absent from Ireland for some time, I have a proposition for you."

Cathal rested his elbows on his desk and his chin on steepled fingers.

"Please. Sit,"

"Are you still agreeable to the offer you made in Wicklow regarding Pride of Tara? If not, I needn't trouble you further."

"The offer still stands Mr. Valentine and will until I can pay off my grandfather's debt to our mutual satisfaction."

"You are a proud man, Cathal O'Neill. I respect that.

"If you are agreeable, I propose taking Ghost to 'Redmile' and using him at stud. Any offspring will be sold by me and any profits split fifty-fifty, as will expenses. That is the broad picture. Of course there will be details to thrash out, but what do you think in principle?"

Cathal spent a moment or two in thought, then the two men got to their feet and firmly shook hands.

"Always assuming we can thrash out the details," Niall laughed. But there was no doubt in either of their minds they would.

I was so delighted for Cathal. Leaving Ghost was always such a wrench, but this way the horse remained his, and the responsibility Mr. Valentine's, leaving him free to manage his American concerns. Generosity bred generosity it seemed - and good will, good will.

It was that same day that Rosie found the O'Neill family portraits on the tower stairs. She fetched me and as usual found the point and got straight to it.

"Who's that, and why is she there?" she asked, pointing at the portrait of the unknown lady set apart from the others.

"I don't know," I said truthfully. I might suspect but I didn't *know*.

Cathal came up behind me and wrapping his arms around my waist, rested his chin on my shoulder.

"None of us know for certain who she is, Rosie. But we suspect her name might have been Caroline Mickley O'Neill, whose nickname was Kitty."

231

"Why?" said Rosie. "Why was she called Kitty if her name was Caroline? Kitty's for Kathleen."

"Or Katharine." I mused.

"Why is she over there? If her name's O'Neil she should be there," Rosie said, pointing at a gap in the portraits next to Seamus the Scar.

"I never thought of that before," said Cathal looking at her in surprise.

Smart cookie, little Rosie Cullen.

Rosalind, hearing the animated conversation, came to stand behind us, smiling benignly at each of us in turn.

"Oh, family portraits - I love them. The ones at 'Redmile' are either incognito or horrible - except for the old ones of the house and grounds."

"Holy crap!" said Rosie, her mother not being present. "Why is your portrait on the wall in an O'Neill house - especially when your Pa hates them so much?"

Tact and Rosie lived in separate houses.

Rosalind had gone as white as a sheet and her mouth had dropped open in astonishment. She turned and ran.

The next thing we heard was an unholy row going on in the sitting room.

Neave turned and we could see she was having problems believing what she was seeing - and hearing.

232

Rosalind, who rarely raised her voice above polite conversation level was laying into her father at the top of her voice.

Then she knocked Neave against the door jamb as she dragged her father by the sleeve down the hall to the tower stairs.

"I've always suspected I was being lied to!" she yelled, crimson-faced. "Why in God's name would you lie to me? I take it my mother's not my mother...., if you see what I mean. Who's that then?"

She pointed a theatrical finger at the offending portrait.

"Who's that? And don't say you don't know. She could be my twin."

There was a deafening silence and it seemed the whole world held its breath.

Niall sat down with a bump on the stairs.

"Do you really want to air our dirty linen in public, daughter?"

"Dirty linen? What bloody dirty linen? Nobody's ever mentioned dirty linen to me! I want this all out in the open and if the only way I can get you to tell the truth is by 'airing our dirty linen' in front of the population of Donegal and Wicklow then... then.."

"So be it?" interjected Rosie helpfully when Rosalind ran out of steam.

Rosalind marched off down the hall like a ship in full sail and sat at the dining room table.

We followed in her wake, and I noticed my littlest sister had the presence of mind to whip the oil painting from the wall and wrap it in her sweater.

Rosalind motioned for her father to sit across the table from her so she could look him square in the eyes. The rest of us filed in and sat wherever there was an available chair.

This was fascinating. It was as if Snow White had suddenly turned into the Wicked Queen.

We waited…., and waited, until finally Niall cracked.

"The picture is of your grandmother, Caroline - Kitty - Mickley O'Neill."

There was a moment's deathly silence then all hell broke loose. Rosalind leapt to her feet.

"Sit DOWN!" she ordered. "Sit DOWN…NOW!"

We sat down - even Cathal and this was his house.

"Edmond - my father - was already in middle-age when he met your grandmother Kitty, and her husband Seamus O'Neill at the Old Horse Fair in Carrickmacross. She was little more than a child.

"She captivated him immediately. It was her expression more than anything else, he used to say. She was very ….."

Niall paused pensively in mid-sentence. Rosalind glowered at him.

"Kitty was gentle and sad, for want of better words.

"Seamus had his Donegal O'Neill lads showing off some pacers he had for sale. Edmond was visiting with Conn Cullen's father who was also selling harness racers. So my father was left squiring Kitty while his friend and Kitty's husband conducted their transactions."

"Stop!" said Neave. "If this is going to be a long session we'll need some refreshments. I won't be long."

I used the break to dash up to my room and fetch the books I'd found in the library. They may be entirely unconnected with Mr. Valentine's account, but I thought they might intrigue him.

Cathal marched Domnall to Jonathan's room at the rear of the house and told him not to let him out of his sight.

Once we had all reassembled in the dining room, Niall with Eefa gazing out of the open sash window, I couldn't help feeling sorry for Mrs. Valentine. She stood outside this tangle too, trying to make sense of it as I was.

Niall returned to the table holding tight to Eefa's hand. It was clear he was finding it difficult and was wondering - as we all were - just who was this virago he'd called daughter all these years, especially when I saw Rosalind, who on a good day might manage a dry sherry, toss back a glass of whisky without turning a hair.

In an effort to gee him along I opened the copy of "Pride and Prejudice" and slid it across the table so both he and Rosalind could see it.

Niall pulled the book towards him and ran his finger over his father's signature, much as I had done.

"I didn't know about this. He must have sent it to her secretly and she hid it. She loved to read. Just an act of kindness to a girl he couldn't help any other way."

It seemed to me the wording of the inscription *"To my most beloved Kitty, Yours, ever in true fidelity..."* spoke of a lot more than a cheer-up for an unhappy young girl. But as the rest of the company were enthralled, I kept my thought to myself.

"Edmond suspected Seamus had been beating Kitty," Niall continued. "My father was a chivalrous man and it broke his heart to see the young woman he had come to care for so mistreated, but he held his tongue not wanting to be seen as coming between a man and his wife.

"The world of horse dealing is a small one and most of the major players are well acquainted.

"Some months later Seamus and my father happened to have business in Wicklow town on the same day.

"Seamus had had a good day and he and his brothers were celebrating in a pub on the town square.

"My father found Kitty sitting on the stone steps of Billy Byrne's statue sobbing her heart out and clutching together her dress, which had been ripped across her breast, one eye blackened and swollen shut. No-one had stopped to help her although the town was teaming with horses and their owners and handlers.

"This was just too much for Edmond. He dragged Seamus from the pub and threatened him with retribution and the constable if he didn't stop abusing his wife.

"Seamus being Seamus told him to 'fuck off' - begging your pardon ladies. His brothers Cormac and Brian swaggered over and stood at his shoulders. The threat was unmistakable."

"What, Uncle Brian? But he was completely harmless. He lived with us until last year, until he…. died," said Neave looking at her brother.

"This was half a century ago Mrs. Cullen - people change.

"My father was not one to be bullied," Mr. Valentine went on. "He stood his ground."

"Remind me again, "what relation was Seamus to you?" Rosalind asked Cathal pointedly.

"He was my grandfather."

Cathal was ashamed beyond bearing and strode from the room, slamming the door behind him.

I left him some much-needed time to himself. He had the old-fashioned pride of an Irish clansman and the stain on his honor was devastating.

"Mr. Valentine," I said firmly. "We can't take on the sins of our fathers, a fact which doesn't appear to have occurred to my husband. If we did, consider the plight of Lizzie Borden's cousin or Ivan the Terrible's aunt."

Everyone grinned, even Mr. Valentine which eased the tension considerably.

All this time Auntie had been unnaturally quiet, and she and Uncle Conn had taken their children and packed them off to bed. Rosheen, I gathered was not happy with her mother, but was told this wasn't Cullen business and she should look to her own concerns.

Rosie had left the little oil painting on the dining table next to Niall Valentine's whisky glass, where he had no chance of missing it.

Cathal returned looking so uncomfortable I could have wept for him. But he was no coward and knew he had to see this through.

There were now seven of us left at the table - Cathal and Neave, and honorary members of the O'Neills by marriage, Daniel and me. Niall and Eefa represented the Valentines. Then there was Rosalind who for the time being was an unknown quantity even to herself.

Niall picked up the little painting and looked at it sadly.

"My father always said the portrait at 'Redmile' did her no justice."

He gazed at the pretty face before continuing:

"When the O'Neill brothers attacked my father they didn't reckon on his sword-stick. Many gentlemen of business in those days carried one for protection; there was little effective law-enforcement at that time.

"In self-defense he slashed at Seamus and caught him across the face. The cut was deep and the brothers were obliged to back down to tend to him.

"My father left before his presence could cause further trouble.

"He had just mounted and was about to ride through the crowds, when he was grabbed by the ankle and to his consternation found himself looking down into the face of Brian O'Neill.

"He was dragging a weeping Kitty behind him by the arm. To my father's surprise, Brian looked over his shoulder, his brother's blood still bright on his shirt, and lifted Kitty onto Edmond's saddle, before disappearing into the throng."

Cathal didn't question the truth of Mr. Valentine's account. But he was at the end of his tether. Nothing further could be accomplished for him that day.

Chapter Forty-seven
Fiona

On the evening of Niall Valentine's revelations, Cathal at my insistence rode the lanes and fields of Donegal until both he and Ghost were exhausted. I took care of the horse and ordered Cathal to bed.

Early next morning we four rode out together across fields wet with dew, the early summer hedgerows resplendent with lacy elderflowers, the verges with cowslips and clover.

With the sun warm on our faces, and thrushes caroling in the trees, it couldn't have been further removed from the trauma we all suspected was about to unfold.

When we entered 'Túr Capaill' Domnall was loading suitcases into the dog-cart and the Cullen family awaited us in the sitting room.

"I'm glad you're back," said Aunt Siobhan. "I told Rosheen yesterday it was O'Neill and Valentine concerns but she won't mind her own business and Rosie... well, you know Rosie. So it's time we were going home."

It struck me forcibly I now had a husband and a new life and no claim on the past. Auntie realized it too and threw her arms round my neck and wept. I knew she felt Daniel and I were lost to her, and I supposed we were.

Leaving Mam and Kitty, Sally and Billy - not to mention Uncle Frank and Polly and Dolly - had cost me no heartache, but this was quite different. These people cared and had given my life back to me.

Uncle Conn who was not only losing a son and an adopted daughter but a stable master and a mucker-out, said through clenched teeth:

"Don't be strangers," then headed for the door.

Daniel and I went out to Cathal's car, ready to go to the station and see them off only to be taken to one side by my aunt.

"The foolish man's just about managing, so better you stay here."

Then she hugged us to her bosom and kissed us tearfully, before climbing into the car. A forlorn Rosie with a trembly chin blew us all kisses.

Cathal started the car and they were gone.

It was mid-afternoon before my husband returned, by which time Neave had had the cook prepare a good old-fashioned stew and uncorked a couple of bottles of Bordeaux.

Nobody was hungry but we ate anyway.

There was no way to avoid the conclusion of Mr. Valentine's saga, so there was a sense of trepidation. I could see Rosalind was set on continuing and much as he might dislike it, it was something Cathal must face.

"Are *you* certain you want to continue Rosalind?" asked Eefa Valentine anxiously. "I do know what happened and it may trouble you. Perhaps it's for the best we stop here."

That was absolutely not going to happen! Everyone ignored her.

Mr. Valentine lit a small cheroot and blew out a swirl of blue smoke.

"Before I continue, please understand that what is to follow was told to me by my father. Now he's no longer with us I have no way of checking its truth."

Niall brushed ash off the sleeve of his jacket.

"It wasn't until Edmond lifted Kitty down from his saddle that he truly understood how badly injured she was.

"He was at his wit's end to know what to do. Your mother, Dan, was working at 'Redmile' at the time. She was only a girl but she had the sense to search out the only person she could think of who might be able to help - Aileen Collins, who became my mother when she married Edmond.

"She was what my grandmother would have called a 'wise woman' - very apt indeed, for that she was. In those days of no doctors she had the skills to help the sick.

"But it was too late. To Father's horror, Kitty was found to be pregnant. My mother hadn't been able to stem the bleeding," he took a deep breath, "but she managed to save the little girl. Father took her in, christened her Fiona Valentine and determined to bring her up as his own, safe and protected from her own blood, Seamus O'Neill.

"And that's were my knowledge ends…

"The only other thing I can tell you with any certainty and for which I have no explanation, is once Fiona was grown, despite the difference in their ages, my father Edmond married her."

Every mouth in the room dropped open.

"Fiona O'Neill was my MOTHER?" demanded Rosalind appalled. Eefa, who she had always believed to be her parent, rushed to comfort her but Rosalind pushed her aside.

"Go on with what you know, Father," she said with determination.

"As I've already said, I know nothing else, but something of importance must have occurred between Edmond and Seamus in the months prior - perhaps that's for Cathal to discover.

"The rest you know. Eefa and I married a few years later and our only child Aidan was born two years after that."

He hugged his wife who was clearly heartbroken.

"Our only child…, Niall. The only one, now gone… all gone."

"Very gratifying," said Rosalind sourly. "I've lived with you all my life. I'd have thought you'd have considered me family by now."

Chapter Forty-eight
Hidden Boxes and Another Train to Dublin

The following morning, Cathal left Jon and Domnall in charge of the horses, while he and I set to to search his office, also used in the past by his father and grandfather and probably generations before that.

His own box-files, neatly labeled and stored on floor to ceiling shelves on both sides of his desk, we left alone.

Whereas many of the little-used rooms in the house were dusty and lackluster, Cathal's office was pristine. His maple -wood desk overlooked the stable yard, a blotter laid squarely on it's top. Work he was currently engaged in lay neatly in folders in one corner and a small metal tray held variously used sticks of sealing wax and a stamp.

Against the wall opposite the door, was an elderly caste-iron security safe with a small ivory plaque attached to its door depicting a Victorian race-horse.

Apart from his own swivel desk chair and a couple of plush seats for visitors, that was it.

Cathal search through his keys and unlocked a door at the back of the room I'd never noticed before.

I got the distinct impression it hadn't been opened since his father died. It smelled unpleasantly musty and had no windows: a long narrow room which ran the width of the office and had wooden shelving stacked high with dusty cardboard boxes.

It took us two days to search every box top to bottom. There was nothing! Not a damn thing.

When we reemerged, Neave who had made it her job to keep us fueled with food and drink, was in the sitting room dancing with an imaginary partner to her phonograph. Daniel was leafing through a magazine.

Cathal and I sat before the fire which burned year round in this ancient house to stave off the damp.

He stared into the crackling embers deep in thought.

"I was sure there'd be something among the business papers belonging to my father and grandfather. Perhaps Dad burned them."

"Is there somewhere else we could try?" I asked. "Seamus's mother commissioned the portraits - she must have known Kitty."

Cathal left the room returning a few moments later hauling the enormous O'Neill family bible.

Neave turned off the phonograph.

"There…" she said, running a neatly manicured finger down the faded page. "There - Seamus O'Neill born June 1st 1841, to Sam and Mary Johns O'Neill."

"Mary built the library too, didn't she?" I asked. "There may be more information concealed there."

We searched the library, the four of us taking down every volume and even rapping on the wainscotting to search for hollow sounds. But there was absolutely nothing at all. Nothing but regular cover prints in the dust on the shelves.

So the mystery seemed likely to remain a mystery. Poor Rosalind might never have the full story of her birth and three days of my life had been used up on this fruitless search. I was going to bed.

In the privacy of our bedroom the fire had burned low in the hearth, reduced to brittle embers. Cathal ran his hands down my arms and entwined our fingers, kissing the rings which bound us.

This particular evening, after I washed off the dust from my hands and face, he sat me in front of my dressing table mirror, unwound my hair and brushed it in long strokes until it gleamed.

The bed was warm and soft and he made love to me with increasing ardor until we both cried out on the same breath, then slept in each other's arms until dawn.

The next morning the Valentines told us over breakfast they too would be leaving.

Mr. Valentine was to set off immediately and ride the width of Ireland taking Ghost back to 'Redmile' as promised.

Cathal spent a distraught morning with his beloved friend and it seemed Ghost felt the same. He was the quietest I'd ever seen him and trotted off with this head bent. Cathal wept openly but by the time they came back a couple of hours later, both seemed to have come to terms with their fate and, if not happy, were at least resigned.

Eefa Valentine and Rosalind were to follow the next day by train and spent the day packing.

Rosalind took the little portrait of her grandmother to the stairs to rehang it, then changed her mind and asked Cathal's permission to take it to 'Redmile'. He readily agreed.

I went with Cathal to see Eefa and Rosalind onto the train. Rosalind looked worn out.

"You will tell me if you find anything else won't you, Bridie?" she said, her brow creased with worry.

"Of course I will," I said, hugging her and kissing her cheek. "This must be so distressing for you. You must tell me too if you find anything which might help."

A stray tear ran down her cheek. She wiped it away and jumped aboard the train just as the station master blew his whistle.

I said nothing but it occurred to me that Niall Valentine was not being entirely honest with his daughter. There was still the question of why she'd been so closely watched her entire life.

With all our guests gone and the house echoing and quiet, we sat before the fire in the sitting room each concerned with his own thoughts. Neave paced back and forth restlessly.

When she left the room, no-one took particular notice. I just thought she'd wanted to be alone and had gone to her room to rest.

For Dan, Cathal and I the mood was one of lethargy after the over-excitement of the past few days.

When Neave hadn't returned within the hour, I took it upon myself to go find her.

My first thought was her parlor - but she wasn't there, although her handiwork was laid neatly beside her chair.

I searched the portrait gallery and library thinking she might have gone there to think. But she wasn't there either.

Next, I tried her room - all the family's rooms were on the first floor. Her door was ajar - she wasn't there, but I heard a rustle and muffled cry which came from a room at the far end of the hall. I might have missed it if a moment later the cry wasn't repeated, a little louder this time."

I dashed down the hall and flung open the door. Neave was sitting on the bed which was strewn with papers and held a dusty file open on her knees.

That it had been Brian's room was immediately apparent. His silver topped cane was propped against a chest of drawers and a cravat was draped over the back of a chair.

Tear-filled eyes wide with shock, she whispered:

"I found them," then louder, "I found them. Seamus's papers. I came up to pack some of Uncle Brian's things to give me something to do. They were stored in a box at the back of his wardrobe."

The box was laying, top askew, on the floor at her feet.

The papers were very old and in some places had worn away altogether. Many were written in indelible pencil, its purple uneven and faded with age. It would take all of us to sort through them, there were so many.

We placed the neatly ordered sheets of paper on the dining table and the four of us spent an hour reordering the documents Neave had strewn across the bed.

The papers were all from the same year, 1879, and each month was filed in a different colored folder.

Mostly they seemed to be bills of sale - dozens of them.

"Look!" said Dan. "Most of the papers I have here are for the Irish army. He must have moved Edmond's horses straight on to the military. They wouldn't have bothered too much about prior ownership."

"But they were thoroughbreds!" I said horrified.

"Officers' mounts," said Cathal. "They would have sorted out the better ones and sold the rest on. Nice nest egg for someone. I don't suppose grandfather would have cared too much what he got for them.

"That tells us where the horses went, but still there are no details of why he behaved as he did. We can go see but I'm almost certain there's nothing left in that room."

Chapter Forty-nine
Uncle Brian's Affairs

The next few days the four of us spent catching up with the delights of married life, and very little time was spent in the downstairs rooms.

Cara, short of anything else to do. took it upon herself to give the library the best clean it'd had since the 1850s.

Domnall was bored stiff since he had no snooping to do - or at least I hoped not - and Jonathan stood twiddling his thumbs waiting for Cathal to give him instructions.

Once we'd all come down off cloud nine, it was time to plan our long overdue honeymoon. Honeymoon I say although I got the impression the Donegal O'Neills wouldn't be prised from the US of A with a crowbar for quite some time to come.

Cathal's business was based over there now, and he was longing to 'get back home'. As he intended passing over the mantle of Chief - literally - to a distant cousin, I had little confidence we'd be back in Ireland any time soon, if at all..

I didn't know how I felt about that. My time in America had hardly been a joyful experience and Ireland was so beautiful and I had been so happy there. On the whole I'd rather have stayed, but Cathal was set on going so I didn't argue.

The days of flappers were now long past, but Neave had managed to turn herself into a pretty good imitation of Katheryn Hepburn, and had perfected the art of mixing Manhattans - 'on the rocks' *and* with a cherry, daarling' -

to a fine art. It would be interesting watching her resume her personal battle with Prohibition.

Neave completed clearing out Brian's room, vigilant for any further paperwork. There wasn't anything.

After that there remained only a couple of major tasks to conclude this side of the Atlantic: to wind up Brian's estate and close up the house, ready for the new occupants.

Cathal rang the family solicitor in Letterkenny and made arrangements to drive over and sign any papers. Then we could be on our way.

I telephoned Rosalind to tell her we'd hit a brick wall with our family investigations and she said her father hadn't come across anything further at 'Redmile' either. So that was that. Poor Rosalind.

Cathal took us all over to Letterkenny with him. It's a beautiful town with a ruined castle, a cathedral and a scenic lake. I suggested to Cathal we should move there instead of America. His only objection was he'd still be in Ireland and his horses in Kentucky.

We all met up again in the Central Bar near the Cathedral. It had been there for over a hundred years and looked it, but there was a good turf fire, a man playing a tin whistle and a landlord with rosy cheeks and a wide smile.

In all the time I'd been in Ireland, I'd never tried the national brew. To the uninitiated I'd say Guinness looks like tar, has a completely unique almost liquorice flavor, and is drunk through a white head smooth as cream. Heaven in a glass.

I was half way through my pint and feeling increasingly cheerful when Cathal reappeared, ordered a beer and sat down.

He was carrying an envelope and a small wrapped box tied with string and dabbed with crimson sealing wax.

He waved the envelope at us.

"Just what you'd expect. Quite a bit of cash he'd squirrelled away over the years and a few personal bequests - he left me his cane," Cathal finished ironically.

He handed the package to Neave. I peeped over her shoulder so I could read the handwritten directions:

'Personal and Private - For the sole attention of Miss Neave O'Neill of 'Túr Capaill'.

'If she hasn't received it within five years of my death it is to be burned unopened by my solicitor Mr. Gurney.'

Neave took it and turned it over in her hands. It was about the same size as a shoe box but heavier. The writing was quite recent and in a formal script in ink.

She began to pry the wax away but Cathal stopped her.

"Don't. You have no idea what it contains. It's apparent Uncle Brian meant it for your eyes only. He may have meant I shouldn't see it either."

We finished our drinks and walked out into a damp afternoon to the sound of a doleful Cathedral bell.

Neave wasn't the world's most patient person. As soon as we got back to the Tower, she disappeared into her parlor with the package and locked the door.

I went to find Cathal. He was sitting on the pile of straw he kept in the corner of Ghost's stall looking miserable.

"I'm going to have to scrub out this stall and put another horse in it soon."

I felt so sorry for him. He may still own Ghost but it wasn't the same when he was all those miles away in County Wicklow.

I sat beside him and he buried his face in my hair, running his fingers through its long strands

"I do so love you, Bridie O'Neill. Thank you for being my wife," he whispered.

"S'okay," I said. "Any time," in an attempt to lighten his mood.

"Come on. Let's go and see if Neave has reappeared and if she can share her grimoire with us," I said, tugging him to his feet.

"How do you know it's a book?"

"I don't. Just looks like one."

Neave was sitting at Cathal's office desk, 'the grimoire' open before her. So it *was* a book after all. It must have been a book of wicked spells because she looked thoroughly spooked and for the moment unable to speak.

"Uh…" she uttered. "Ummm…errr.."

"Saints preserve us Neave. Do I need to fetch the priest for an exorcism? Has the devil got your tongue?" asked Cathal with the lack of sympathy only a brother could display.

She pointed at the book mutely, so I picked it up.

On the flyleaf was written:

"A Private and Personal Record of the Doings of the O'Neills of Donegal and the Valentines of 'Redmile' in the County of Wicklow, by the last of his generation, Brian Johns O'Neill of 'Túr Capaill'

"Oh, my Good God, Cathal," I said, flicking through the pages. "The rest of the story - or more of it anyway."

Chapter Fifty
Brian's Deathbed Declaration

This time Neave gave the staff the day off and sent Domnall to visit his mother in a neighboring village.

She sat down to read Brian's diary which left the rest of us hopping from one foot to the other.

"Neave - your brother is going to die of apoplexy if you read to the end without letting him look too."

Indeed, Cathal did look hot and bothered. I pulled up a chair, sat him on it and Neave pushed the open book so they could both see it.

He turned over the first page. There was a heading:

"For my beloved Neave, who cared for a crazy old man in his dotage. I hope this may serve to exonerate me a little in your eyes, dear child."

Dan and I took a long walk in wet weather just to calm our agitation and to give Cathal and Neave a little private time to peruse the diary.

When we were soaked to the skin we went back, dried off and fixed some hot tea.

I had been surprised at the affection in that first line from a crazy old coot with a penchant for smoked fish. Now I came to think of it though, where he exasperated Cathal and made him feel guilty, Neave had always treated him with benign humor. Perhaps she had loved him in her own way - perhaps that was the only solace he could take.

I took a tray to the office where they were still deep in concentration turning over page after page, and quietly left.

Neave and Cathal didn't reappear until early evening, by which time my spouse looked ready to drop, and Neave's eyes were puffy and wet with tears.

Of course they may not tell us anything at all, but by the look of them both, they needed Dan's support and my own desperately, so that was unlikely.

"You will understand," said Cathal earnestly, "Neave and I find this distressing."

"Of course you do," I said, holding his hand. "How could it be otherwise?"

"I'll give you a resume - you can read the detail for yourself after if you wish," he said.

"Some things we already know, such as Seamus's beating of Kitty. Brian loved his brother but couldn't condone him beating a helpless innocent so he spirited her away to Edmond for her safety.

"We also know of Fiona's birth and that Edmond later married her. As his wife, Seamus would have no legal access to his own daughter.

"This infuriated grandfather to the point where he determined to ruin Edmond Valentine and take possession of his child," added Neave.

"It didn't take long for Seamus to find Edmond's Achilles heel," Cathal continued. "Edmond's wealth lay in his stock and his land. That particular year, there had been an outbreak of equine 'flu on his farm."

Dan recognized the problem but Cathal explained to me:

"It's not usually fatal but it's highly contagious, so the farm had been quarantined,

"This meant he had outgoings but no income for almost two years and had to take a number of bank loans to get by. When the sickness didn't subside after the first year, he was obliged to remortgage 'Redmile' to pay off the loans. Even this money eventually ran out and the banks began to issue foreclosure notices.

"Edmond became resigned to losing his whole life's work, when who should pop up but Seamus O'Neill."

"Grandfather always had cash and to spare," said Neave with distaste. "As you can see he spent nothing on this place."

"He was a dealer not a breeder so his stock turnover was high," Cathal explained. "He was also unscrupulous, as you've heard. Even his own brother couldn't condone his viciousness, but it would have been more than Brian's life was worth to stand up to him.

"The long and short of it is Seamus paid off Edmond's loans and took his horses in lieu. As an added insult, he left behind on the kitchen table the deeds to 'Redmile' and a signed contract relinquishing ownership of the Valentine lands. He had no need of them and it was a way to boast of his own riches to a man he'd stripped of his whole reason for being.

"Edmond was left with an expensive farm and large house to run, still with no finance. In other words he still had no stock and financially he'd be back where he started, but this time his credit was shot. Punishment indeed.

"Seamus's very worst action was to hamstring Dempsey's Marauder and leave him to bleed to death in his stall. It was this mindless cruelty which destroyed all hope of redemption in Brian's eyes," wept Neave, her respect for her uncle rekindling. She blew her nose loudly.

"You already know Ghost's history. I hadn't been aware of any of this detail. Only that I have always felt it to be true that Ghost didn't belong to the O'Neill's and should be returned to his owner," said Cathal gravely. Then:

"Edmond Valentine was a good man, admired and liked by his fellow breeders and neighbors alike. What's more, it was clear Brian had a great deal of respect for the man he'd trusted with Kitty's life.

"Edmond was particularly close to his neighbors, the Cullens.

"Conn's father, Michael Cullen was instrumental in putting Edmond back on his feet after the bankruptcy. Edmond still possessed Dempsey's King, and his dam, missed by Seamus when he acquired the herd.

"They worked out a plan whereby Edmond would be able to use Dempsey's King to cover borrowed mares from which he would be permitted to keep the offspring. A limit of eight years was attached to the deal.

"Michael took out a mortgage on 'Long Barrow' to finance Edmund's upkeep for the first couple of years.

"Niall had come into his own by now. He was an intelligent man, quick to learn and physically strong. His father was lucky to have him."

Daniel's ears had pricked up at the mention of his grandfather.

"How the hell did Brian O'Neill know all this? He had nothing to do with the Valentines except through Seamus. Da and Mam have never even hinted at any such connection."

"You know your mother minds her own business. Look how she dragged Rosheen off home when she thought she was prying." I said to Dan.

"I can only tell you what's in the diary. You already know as much as I do about the rest," said Cathal shrugging his shoulders.

Neave went on to the part which given her nature would have interested her most:

"In the middle of all this, it seems odd that Seamus had forgotten the source of Edmond's troubles - Kitty and Fiona, the blood daughter Seamus had never clapped eyes on.

"Edmond kept Fiona well-hidden at 'Redmile', such was his fear for her safety if my own family got their hands on her.

"The O'Neill brothers weren't seen in the circles the Valentines moved in for years, and everyone began to feel safe. Then they turned up at Carrickmacross Fair again.

Edmond wasn't there but Michael Cullen saw them, drunk as lords in Monaghan Street at the day's end.

"Here…. look," said Neave, holding out the diary for me to see.

"Seamus, Cormac and me, having sold off our stock, ended up at Finnigans. When we were on our way to being well and truly oiled, I saw Mick Cullen checking his horse's girth across the street. I said naught to Seamus and next time I looked he was gone."

Neave took my arm and continued the account:

"The next person to see Seamus was an acquaintance of Niall's from Wicklow town who saw him at the Horse Fair in Dublin. Carrackmacross was one thing, but Dublin was only thirty miles away. This was getting too close for comfort."

She pushed the book back my way.

"I rode the thirty miles from Wicklow to the Valentine place in an afternoon and warned the man Seamus was on to him and knew he had his own flesh and blood, his daughter imprisoned. He meant to get her back as soon as he'd finish business in Dublin. Meantime he sent me to detain them both for his arrival.

"But this was Kitty's daughter, an innocent babe - she didn't deserve a bastard like Seamus in her life. Liam only survived because he was his father's best harness racer. But a little girl might end up beaten senseless like her mother before her.

"I let them give me the slip. I didn't know the lengths Edmond would go to."

"He married her as Niall said. Now we know why. She was no longer an O'Neill but a Valentine. The Bible makes no mention of her," said Cathal, running his finger down the names on the front page. "She might be this 'rumor', I suppose."

"She was twenty-three," mused Neave, "and he must have been...., damn... old enough to be her father. He was sixty."

"I never saw them again," the diary continued, *"but I did hear there was a baby girl of the marriage. I know no other."*

"We know that was Rosalind from Mr. Valentine's account," I pointed out.

The whole room went silent. You could have heard a pin drop.

"OH MY GOD, Cathal!" screeched Neave, swallowing an entire tumbler of whisky and wiping her hand over her mouth. "Rosalind's our cousin! Look - Seamus is her grandfather!"

"GODDAM so she is!" I said. "Seamus and Kitty were parents to Fiona, Rosalind's mother, and he's your grandfather by his son Liam. *That makes you first cousins!*"

That was all that was said for at least five minutes. Cathal gazed stunned from the window, Neave stoked the fire and I... well, I don't remember what I did.

I didn't spoil it by pointing out that Cathal's mother wasn't the same as Rosalind's, making them as far as I could make out half-first cousins, if there is such a thing. I doubt anyone would have cared - chop the half off and you've got first cousins. That would do.

Dan began to laugh. He laughed until tears were coursing down his cheeks. Neave had to slap his back to stop him choking, and I took him a glass of soda water from the syphon on the tray.

"So what's so bloody funny," glowered Neave.

Danny was looking at Cathal who stared back in alarm.

"You've been fretting for months - years for all I know - about that damn horse and you've given Ghost into the keeping of your uncle by marriage! You couldn't make that up!" and he began to laugh again. "You didn't know he existed two years ago!"

"Well five, actually but I take your point."

Neave fetched another bottle to celebrate, fired up the Marconiphone and we swung round the room to Benny Goodman until we were hot and exhausted.

Dan collapsed into a chair and exclaimed:

"Well, fuck me....!"

His wife hit him over the head with a cushion.

Chapter Fifty-one
A New Cousin Discovered and a Sad Parting for Dan

There wasn't much whoopee made in the O'Neill room that night. We were both so stunned we fell straight to sleep.

I woke up with a feeling something was just not right and walked round the room cleaning my teeth whilst Cathal came to.

"Something's wrong," I frowned. "Something's missing."

He turned over and hid his head under the pillow.

"You didn't call Rosalind last night. I wondered when you'd notice," he said, his voice muffled beneath the bedding.

"Oh yes!" I said, snapping my fingers. "But it's your job now, cuz."

He groaned.

But he needn't have worried. By the time we arrived down for breakfast, Neave had already called 'Redmile' with the news. She stood fingers clasped behind her back fairly seething with excitement.

"I hope you broke it to her gently," I said glaring at her and knowing there wasn't a chance in hell of that. "It's an awful lot for her to take in."

"Oh, she didn't …. take it all in, I mean. But she was SO excited - so pleased. About our bit anyway. I don't think she was too impressed by having Seamus's blood in her veins. She says she'd like to speak to you, Cathal."

She paused and looked wounded.

"I'd already told her everything. Why would she want to speak to you?"

"Because he's her cousin too, dummy," I said as if it was the most obvious thing in the world, whereas in fact I still hadn't come to terms with it myself.

Rosalind was more stunned than pleased. Still, she'd gained family she'd never known she had. Surely it would give her more freedom from her father - after all, she was now not only related to the Valentines, but to the 'O'Neill threat' so her safety was doubly assured.

Cathal took the receiver from my hand and asked to speak to Niall, who had only been given the garbled version from an over-excited Neave and his dumbfounded daughter, so Cathal passed on a more lucid account.

Mr. Valentine asked Cathal if at some point he would mind him taking a look at the original diary.

"I can do better than that, Sir," said Cathal. "With your agreement I'll send my business associate, Jonathan Grainger with it. He can look in on Ghost at the same time.

"Jonathan will be remaining behind to wind up some outstanding business while I take Bridie on her long-awaited honeymoon to New York, so I must leave the matter in your hands - and Jon's - for the time being.

"Regarding Pride of Tara - Ghost - I can find no documentation linking him to his grandsire, Dempsey's Marauder so his lineage is now untraceable."

Cathal nuzzled my cheek affectionately, "You will appreciate my wife and I have business of our own to conclude."

"Indeed... yes, indeed you do! And Daniel and Neave too, I would imagine."

Jonathan Grainger eventually lost patience with his boss's complicated affairs and left for 'Redmile' by train a day earlier than planned. He carried the diary, a letter outlining the Valentine and O'Neill history and a three volume first edition of 'Pride and Prejudice' addressed to Miss Molly Cullen of 'Long Barrow' Farm.

Cathal sent Domnall too - a smart move since my husband was sure to hear back absolutely every detail of the visit with or without Jon's permission.

Domnall was delighted at the prospect of the train journey - Jonathan less so.

Dan and I looked on in amazement as the O'Neill siblings set to organizing our journey to America.

Within the week, the tickets were booked and Neave had packed everything but the kitchen sink into two trunks - one for herself and Dan and one for Cathal and me.

We left everything else. When - if - we did come back it wouldn't be to this house. This now belonged to Keiran O'Neill of the town of Ballyshannon who had taken over as Chief.

Cathal said Ballyshannon was a beautiful place surrounded by rivers and waterfalls. What in God's name Keiran would make of 'Túr Capaill' I couldn't begin to imagine.

The day before we were due to leave, I found Danny sitting on a dry-stone wall near the Tower gate. He looked absolutely miserable.

"You look as if you've lost a dollar and found a dime," I said, putting my arm round his shoulders. "What's wrong?"

In that moment I saw a side of him I'd never appreciated before. He was as Irish as the ground we walked on, a tragic, romantic figure about to be uprooted and truly floundering.

"What's wrong, Danny?" I asked more sympathetically.

"When you and I went to New York last time, I always thought I'd come back home again.

"But this time, I feel I may never see Mam and Da again. Rosie will never run rings round me, Ronan will never play his drum. I won't see Rosheen grow more beautiful by the day. If Neave and I have babes, the chances are they'll never know their Aunt Molly or Uncle Sean. I don't know if I can go."

To my utter amazement, tears began to stream down his cheeks. I let him cry. When he collected himself again I said:

"I guess it's called growing up, Dan. Soon we'll no longer be the youngest generation. Forgetting the past is something I've had to get used to before, but it's new to you."

"But can I, Bridie - can I go?"

"Your choice I guess boils down to Cordonagh or Neave. I'll leave you to mull it over."

Five minutes later he was kissing his wife in the hall, cabin bag at their feet packed and ready.

Danny opened dreamy eyes over Neave's shoulder and said:

"I shall just have to work hard at being a success. Then I can see Mam whenever I want."

Chapter Fifty-two
Return to Byrne Avenue

Cathal, who'd been leaning against the sitting room door jamb listening to the exchange, whispered in my ear:

"I'd already planned to make him my go-between with Niall Valentine. I intend buying stock from him for Lexington.."

I once remarked that Neave could charm the birds from the trees. It seemed it was a family trait - well, this generation of it anyway.

"I got you this," he said, and I saw the glint of gold between his fingers… goddam and blast it - a small plain gold cross.

History repeating itself! If it had Lorelei on the back I'd strangle him with it.

Of course it didn't. It was engraved on the reverse with: *"God Alone Knows"* which I thought was beautifully enigmatic. "..how much I love you," he whispered.

The trip across the Atlantic was…, a trip across the Atlantic. What more can I say? This was my fourth time so its excitement had worn off - I was becoming quite cosmopolitan.

It was hard not to be caught up in Neave's enthusiasm for shopping though. Even a trip via England couldn't dampen her spirits. Her spouse looked like wilted lettuce by the time we disembarked at the Port of New York.

"Never mind, husband," said Neave. "The Cotton Club opens seven days a week. We'll catch it tomorrow. Won't that be interesting?"

"Knock it off, Neave," said her brother. "You'll scare the poor guy to death."

The Americanisms where flying fast now we were back on my native soil!

"Are you rich, Cathal?" I thought to ask, although it had never occurred to me before.

"Comfortable," he said, flicking the ash from his cigarette into a marble ashtray and burying his head further into his copy of the New York Times.

Strange that he became a different person when he left Ireland - more urbane and charming. Both sides of him seemed to love me so I didn't really care - and I was rather partial to both sides of him too.

We spent time alone strolling through Central Park and laughed about which of the extravagant automobiles on Fifth Avenue Cathal would buy me, to match the mink coat design I'd seen on a fancy display in Macy's.

"Any, so long as it's the right shade of pink," he said, mimicking my speech like a magpie.

All too soon it was time for the men to get back to business and Daniel and Cathal set off for Lexington where they were to meet Jonathan.

We girls toyed with the idea of visiting South America in the meantime, but when Neave mentioned it on the telephone to Daniel - tongue in cheek - it was Cathal's voice I heard from across the room.

"The fuck they will! Rio de Janeiro? You can't even drink the bloody water there!" He'd grabbed the receiver from Daniel mid-sentence.

"I'd thought further north - Peru perhaps," I teased. "I thought a visit to that place in the mountains - the ruin they dug up recently. Can't remember its name. What's it called, Neave?"

"Machu Picchu," she said absently, concentrating on filing a fingernail.

Cathal was spluttering on the other end of the line.

"You will NOT. I will NOT hear of it. Do you understand me Bridie?"

"Moot point Cathal since you and Dan are eight hundred miles away. Fancy going Neave?"

"Sure thing."

Dan and Cathal were on the doorstep two days later.

Neave ushered them into the sitting room, brows raised, and china blue eyes wide and innocent.

"Whatever are you doing here? We weren't expecting you - you could have given us some notice. Did you know about this?" she asked me as I walked through the door.

"Certainly not. I would have told you."

"We've been had," said Dan to Cathal.

Cathal, taut with frustration picked up the jacket he'd flung over a chair and marched out of the door to the little park across the road.

"Can't do it Neave," I said.

"No staying power!"

We both fell about laughing.

I skipped between the automobiles and flopped onto the park bench next to him.

."Idiot!" I said. "How can you believe all that crap? Neave and I were just playing. We never in this world expected you to fall for it.

"I promise I will never go anywhere without you," I said seriously. "From now on I'll stick to you like glue... see how you like *that*!"

For all our lives, I hoped he would kiss me as he did in that moment.

Epilogue
Part One

Danny, Cathal and Jonathan Grainger made a formidable business team which is why I am now lazing on a chaise longue beside an open French window, watching my beloved school a beautiful bay horse.

My cousin and sister-in-law lived in an enchanting cottage Cathal had built to their design on our ranch and Jonathan was close by in urban Frankfort.

As promised, Cathal had used Dan and Jonathan to do the travelling back and forth to Ireland. That way Conn and Siobhan were able to hold their oldest child, his wife and little son often.

I understood from Daniel, Rosalind was being drawn into the blue-eyed gaze of that charmer Jonathan Grainger, her cousin's man of business. I just hoped her father would be kind.

Cathal and I now had a beautiful daughter of our own - the third generation Rosie. She hadn't inherited the O'Neill red hair but had chestnut curls like the impudent aunt she was named after. And so naughty!

One night when she was three years old, Cathal called out the entire staff to search for her and found her fast asleep, under a pile of straw in an empty stall. She'd a wet thumb stuck in her mouth and was clinging tight to a curry comb.

Instead of being furious, Cathal tossed her in the air and yelled:

"Who's daddy's princess? We'll make an Olympian of you yet. What do you fancy? Dressage or the jumps?

"Drethage."

Then to me he said with no attempt at tact:

"Come on - let's make another."

Dumping Rosie into the nearest pair of arms, he dragged me into the house, up the stairs and proceeded to do just that. We named him Edmond.

Epilogue
Part Two

One day when Rosie had just turned six and Edmond was two, Cathal returned all fired up from a business trip to New York.

He'd called from Cincinnati on the way and told me to leave Ed with Neave and throw some things in a bag for me and Rosie - he'd be picking us up in an hour - optimistic even if he swam the Ohio, but I did as I was asked.

He drove like an idiot back to New York, screeching to a halt before 18 Byrne Avenue.

At this point I told him to get a hold of his enthusiasm. His daughter was exhausted and her mother pretty much the same.

I tucked Rosie up in our bed and watched Cathal jump from chair to sitting room chair.

"What in God's name's gotten into you? You're wearing holes in Neave's Axminster! Sit down!"

He walked back and forth a few times, downed a couple of shots of whisky, walked a bit more then collapsed onto the sofa next to me.

"I've a surprise for you tomorrow. Please don't ask me what it is - it'll spoil everything."

"Okay, I won't."

"I mean it - please don't ask!"

"Me too. I won't."

In the end I crawled into bed with Rosie and he slept on the sofa.

The following morning, Cathal charged into the bedroom looking like an unmade bed himself and flung wide the curtains.

"Up, up - or it'll be too late!"

Rosie looked at me for reassurance that this was indeed her father and not some random lunatic.

"It's okay, Honey. He'll come back to us eventually," I said - but he was already gone.

I got us both up and dressed and was surprised to be met in the hall by Dan and Neave.

"Who's looking after Ed?"

"Your housekeeper," said Neave.

"Do you have the first idea what's going on?" I asked. "He's gone completely crazy - it's like living with Coco the Clown."

"Nope," said my sister-in-law with no interest whatever.

Cathal and Dan, who *did* seem to know what was happening, marched us a couple of miles across depressingly grey streets until we reached a place which looked familiar, but I just couldn't figure where I'd seen it before.

Danny took hold of my hand - which was strange in itself - and walked me round the corner.

I gasped in horror.

Laid out before us in serried ranks were row after row of gutted tenements, the windows - glassless - stared blankly outwards, with the occasional remains of a torn and blackened lace curtain blowing in a gentle breeze. Some of the lower windows had been partially sealed with sheets of corrugated-iron which had fallen from the stories above, smashing into everything in their way and scattering already-disintegrating bricks against a road of uneven cobbles.

Dungannon Road.

And standing like a crooked finger in the middle of all the filth and decay stood the very lamp post where Jimmy Dobson's leg had parted company with the rest of him.

I didn't know whether to laugh or cry. Daniel took my hand.

"We can leave now if you'd rather," he said quietly. "It's been standing empty for years but today they're beginning to demolish it. You said goodbye to your memories here when you left with me. We thought you might like to lay *all* your specters to rest."

I pulled away and dream-walked, staggering occasionally over debris, to the top of the road. It was full of grey ghosts.

Mam, laughing and tottering slightly from the contents of the bottle in her apron pocket; a scream as we found Pa's body suspended from the ceiling; another when Jimmy collided with the tatter's cart. The apparition of a New York taxi from which jumped a funny little man in tight vest and baggy trousers - my savior had I but known it.

I walked a little further.

There was Carter's Yard where the ghost of Michael Cullen O'Neill was laying into Lilian Greenwood with gusto and our Kitty was peeping round the corner.

I was about to turn into Dean Street. I had the impression that Old Man Greenwood's hardware store would still be standing neat as a new pin as always amidst all this carnage.

"Mommmeeee!"

I was brought back to myself by my daughter's anguished cry and swung up into my husband's strong arms. He ran down the road with me, leaping old planks and half-collapsed walls to safety.

We had just reached our vantage point when an enormous concrete ball shattered a hole in what may have been the Shamrock Ale House of years ago.

In slow motion, a domino effect tumbled tenement wall against tenement wall, the action ending in an ear-shattering crash and a great cloud of grime.

I stood for a few more minutes, my past life playing like a movie behind my eyes, then turned my back and lifted my daughter - a little innocent as I had been, playing hop-scotch on nearby chipped paving slabs soon to be gone forever.

"Come on, Rosie-posie - let's get an ice cream," I said.

Printed in Great Britain
by Amazon

14126471R00163